Did he still love

The question echoed in her mind as he scooped her into his arms and carried her into the ER.

"Put me down. I can walk on my own."

She was used to being strong, carrying her own load. She took care of people, not the other way around.

"Maybe you ought to admit that you can't do everything alone," he said. "You should accept help and say thank you."

"Back at you, buddy," she said.

At her comment, his jaw hardened, but he didn't reply.

"Why do you keep shutting me out?" she asked. "You need me. Can't you admit it?"

He met her eyes. Maybe she shouldn't have said that, but lately she'd been thinking it was true. That maybe it had been a mistake to let him break up with her.

But a second chance with Sean? It was a risk she didn't know if her heart could take.

Leigh Bale is a *Publishers Weekly* bestselling author. She is the winner of the prestigious Golden Heart® Award and is a finalist for the Gayle Wilson Award of Excellence and the Booksellers' Best Award. The daughter of a retired US forest ranger, she holds a BA in history. Married in 1981 to the love of her life, Leigh and her professor husband have two children and two grandkids. You can reach her at leighbale.com.

Books by Leigh Bale

Love Inspired

Men of Wildfire

Her Firefighter Hero
Wildfire Sweethearts

Lone Star Cowboy League

A Doctor for the Nanny

The Healing Place
The Forever Family
The Road to Forgiveness
The Forest Ranger's Promise
The Forest Ranger's Husband
The Forest Ranger's Child
Falling for the Forest Ranger
Healing the Forest Ranger
The Forest Ranger's Return
The Forest Ranger's Christmas
The Forest Ranger's Rescue

Wildfire
Sweethearts

Leigh Bale

(H) **HARLEQUIN**® LOVE INSPIRED®

Recycling programs for this product may not exist in your area.

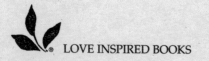

LOVE INSPIRED BOOKS

ISBN-13: 978-0-373-62270-2

Wildfire Sweethearts

www.Harlequin.com

Printed in U.S.A.

Peace I leave with you, my peace I give unto you: not as the world giveth, give I unto you. Let not your heart be troubled, neither let it be afraid.
—*John* 14:27

This book is dedicated to the Stanislaus Interagency Hotshot Crew. Thanks so much for your hospitality when I came to visit your home base. I learned so much in that short time and enjoyed every moment. Stay safe out there!

And many thanks to Greg and JoAnn Overacker. Your expertise and knowledge of wildfire fighting astound me. How I wish my husband and I lived nearby so we could meet and chat over dinner with you on a regular basis. You are two of the warmest, most generous people I've ever met.

Any errors in this book are mine alone.

Chapter One

Tessa Carpenter stared with dismay at the drafts of gray smoke billowing from the engine of her beat-up old truck.

Correction. Zach's truck. Even though her elder brother had died last summer, she would never sell his truck, even if it did qualify for the scrap pile.

Cruising down the highway at sixty-five miles per hour, she tapped the brake to decrease her speed. The moving trailer attached to the back hitch trembled slightly. It held all her worldly possessions. Clothes, books, bedding, her firefighting pack and her precious picture albums. Not a lot, but she didn't want to lose any of it.

She gripped the steering wheel as the vehicle slowed. Edging over onto the shoulder, she killed the engine. As she thrust open the heavy door, she caught the acrid scent of burning oil. Her nose twitched with repugnance and she got out to inspect the problem.

Great! Just great. If it was a flat tire, no big deal. She could change that in a heartbeat. She'd done it before. Many times, in fact. But truck engines? She didn't have a clue. As the only woman on the Minoa Inter-agency Hotshot crew, she could do anything the guys could do. It was just a matter of patience and leverage. But engines were not her forte. Never had been, never would be. She was better at numbers and always ended up doing the inventory reports instead.

She rested her hands on her hips. Turning her face into the fresh April breeze, she took a deep inhale then blew it out in an irritable sigh. She was officially stranded on Highway 50, halfway between the sleepy mining towns of Eureka and Austin, Nevada. It wasn't called the Loneliest Road in America for nothing. Her gaze took in miles of brown hills, sage and rabbit brush. Not a single building or car in sight.

Well, no sense standing here gawking. Hotshots were people of action. It could always be worse. At least it wasn't raining. And while the spring weather was un-seasonably warm, it could be a whole lot hotter, too.

She popped the hood to the engine then jumped back as she was engulfed in a cloud of smoke. She couldn't tell where it came from and wondered if the truck had overheated, or if it had a more serious issue.

Reaching into the pocket of her blue jeans, she pulled out her cell phone and entered her security number. A huff of impatience whooshed from her throat. No connectivity out here in the middle of nowhere. She'd have to wait for someone to come along. Which could take hours.

So much for her plans to arrive in Minoa early enough to unpack and settle into her furnished apart-ment before driving thirty miles to Carson City to re-turn the mover's trailer. Minoa was too small a town to have a truck rental business. As long as she turned the trailer in by tomorrow night at seven o'clock, she wouldn't have to pay any late fees. But she'd be in deep kimchi if she didn't report for her first day back at work tomorrow morning.

Leaving the hood up to signal for help, she climbed inside the truck and lowered the windows to catch the mild breeze blowing across the Nevada desert. She stared out her windshield, wishing she had a book to read. Reaching for the water bottle she'd stowed in the cup holder an hour earlier, she popped the lid and took a deep swallow before setting the bottle aside.

She had just dozed off when the low thrum of an approaching vehicle brought her back to the present. A shiny blue pickup truck pulled up behind her. In the side mirror, she caught the flash of a tall, well-built man getting out and walking toward her. Dressed in faded blue jeans, his long legs moved in a self-assured stride. But something familiar about that muscular physique caused her to narrow her eyes.

No, it couldn't be.

Her pulse sped up into double-time, her breath rushing out in a lung-squeezing sigh. A warm, tingly sensation flowed over her as she tilted her head to get a better look in her rearview mirror.

"Oh, no." She leaned her forehead against the steering wheel and groaned.

Sean Nash. Her ex-fiancé. Except for her brother, he was the only man she'd ever loved. Okay, that wasn't entirely true. She'd loved her father once, before he'd abandoned her family when she was only seven years old. But that was so long ago that she barely remembered him.

Standing beside her door, Sean angled his face toward her and flashed a dimpled smile. A smile that still turned her brains to mush.

"Hi, there. I didn't expect to meet you all the way out here in the middle of nowhere." His voice sounded low and reserved. No doubt he was surprised to see her, too.

"Likewise," she said, wondering what he was doing here.

"Looks like you've got some car trouble," he said.

Morning sunlight sprayed across his too-broad shoulders, highlighting his short, curly hair. He shifted his weight in a careless, confident stance that told her he knew how to handle himself in any situation. Except she knew that wasn't true.

A lance of anger speared her, but she ignored it. He'd always been in charge. Always demanding the best out of his crew. So calm under pressure. Never needing anyone. Not even God. But when she thought of how their relationship had fallen apart, she didn't know how Sean could act so cool and remote around her. Not when her entire body was trembling with emotion.

"Something's the matter with the engine," she said.

Warring sentiments fogged her brain. Relief, anger and sorrow. She wrestled to make sense of it all and tried to maintain her composure. After all, he'd been the one to break off their engagement. The day after her brother's funeral, he'd taken her for a quiet ride in his truck. He'd parked beneath the shade of an elm tree on the outskirts of town and stared out the window as he'd told her that he didn't want to marry her anymore. She knew he was hurting over Zach's death. They both were. But she thought they could comfort one another. Unfortunately, he didn't see it that way. He'd suffered smoke inhalation, torn ligaments, shock and second-degree burns. They'd postponed the funeral until he was released from the hospital. In the chaos of comforting her distraught mother, nursing her own grief and making burial arrangements, Tessa had spent long hours sitting by Sean's bedside. But the day after the funeral, he had told her that his change of heart had nothing to do with Zach. That his priorities had simply changed and he wanted to move on. His plans no longer included her.

We're not right for each other. I don't want to marry you now.

The sting of those words still haunted her, like a sliver lodged in her heart. He didn't want her anymore.

Unfortunately, she was now stranded and needed Sean's help. She couldn't see his eyes through his dark sunglasses. She hated when he wore them because she couldn't read the emotions on his face. A face she knew as well as her own. The high forehead, saber-sharp cheekbones, stubborn chin and translucent blue eyes that pierced her to the core every time he looked at her. Handsome, with a careless smile that could scorch her toes to ash. But something was different about him. Something that hadn't been there before Zach's death. Something she couldn't quite put a finger on.

Wearing a white T-shirt and boots, Sean still looked lean, strong and ready for action. Considering they both fought wildfires for a living and he'd been a squad leader on her crew last season, she figured he was dressed appropriately. It suited his personality. Rugged and masculine. Always prepared. Always in control.

Until the day Zach had died.

Sean stepped back as she opened the door. She climbed out, trying not to look at him. Trying not to let his presence undermine her composure. He was the last person she'd expected to see on this deserted road. Unfortunately, this was the main road heading from Ely to Reno. The only road, unless she wanted to drive on dirt and go four-wheeling.

"What are you doing all the way out here?" she asked, catching his scent. A subtle mixture of spicy cologne and licorice candy.

He gave a lazy shrug. "Driving to Minoa, the same as you."

"After last fire season, I thought you were planning to move to Idaho. You said you were putting in on a fire control management job in Boise," she said.

"No, I decided to wait a bit longer."

Wait for what? The job had surely closed by now and he'd lost his window of opportunity. Frankly, she doubted he'd like being cooped up in a stuffy office anyway. He'd always preferred working out in the field, where the action was.

"So, you've been living in Minoa since last summer?"

Most hotshots like her were seasonal employees, working April through August. But Sean had been a permanent hire with benefits, working twelve months out of the year.

"Yeah, I took a short leave of absence from work, but I've been back for five months now. Why?" A thatch of curly black hair fell over his high forehead. Hair she used to thread her fingers through.

"Where have you been? Today, I mean, since you're out here on this road." It was too much of a coincidence that he happened to come upon her on this lonely highway, wasn't it?

"At a training exercise in Utah."

Hmm. She wondered if one of their mutual friends had told him that she'd be traveling this road today.

After all that had happened, she couldn't believe he still wanted to fight wildfire. But it seemed to be in his blood. He was good at it, too. None better. An adrenaline junkie who thrived on the action. With no family of his own, he had nothing to lose. A man who acted first and thought about the dangers later.

After Sean had broken her heart, she'd never wanted to see him again. But here he was, bigger than life. And now it appeared that they'd be working together once more. Which made her hands sweat and her stomach feel queasy. If she'd known he was still here, she would have found other employment, on a different hotshot crew in another state. Now it was too late. Because she needed this job. Badly.

Working on this team would give her the firefighting experience she needed to reach her career goals of one day becoming a fire management officer with the Forest Service. Also, the money would pay her college tuition in the fall. Just one more year of schooling and she'd have her master's degree in resource conservation with a minor in fire science.

She took a deep inhale and let it go, resigned to working with Sean again. If she could fight fire, she could certainly handle this. He was on a different squad than she was and she could keep her distance. If she could just make it through the next five months, she'd never have to see him again. She'd finish school then get a job somewhere far away from his brooding smile and penetrating eyes—and her bittersweet memories.

Without permission, he hopped up into the back of her truck and rummaged around in Zach's silver toolboxes. Tessa didn't complain. Over the years, Sean had spent as much time in this rusty vehicle as she had.

"You got any water?" Clutching several tools, Sean jumped down and sauntered toward the front fender. Tough and agile, his body moved with the feline grace of a star athlete.

For several pounding moments, her gaze followed him as he propped his sunglasses on top of his head. He looked good. Too good. But he was thinner than she remembered, and deeper worry lines creased the corners of his eyes. Eyes that now seemed so sad and empty.

She hadn't seen him in eight months, and it had given her time to think. Breaking up with her so suddenly didn't make sense. She could understand Sean changing his priorities. Life and death situations had a way of making a person reevaluate what they really wanted. But it had cut her deeply to know that he no longer wanted her. It had also made her slightly suspicious. He'd been cleared of any wrongdoing in Zach's death, but what if he was responsible somehow? Had he broken up with her out of guilt? Or was he just afraid of loving and losing her the way he'd lost Zach? Maybe there was some other reason she didn't understand?

Reaching inside the cab, she retrieved her half-empty water bottle. When she returned, Sean was bent over the engine like a pro mechanic. His expressive eyes crinkled as he squinted against the bright sunlight. Without looking up, he shot a hand out and she placed the bottle in his grasp.

Copying his manners, she shook her head. He was still the same old Sean she'd known for nine years. Her brother's best friend. Tough and proud. Never mincing words.

If only he hadn't shut her out. If only she knew what had really happened that fateful day when her brother died. After some time had passed, she'd been hoping Sean might call her to talk about Zach's death, but he hadn't opened up one bit. As it stood, he'd broken her heart and she no longer trusted him.

"What do you think the matter is?" She ducked her head and peered at the engine.

"It's overheated."

"Obviously. But is it serious?"

"We'll know in a moment."

Wrapping a handful of his shirttail around his fingers to protect against burns, Sean twisted off the cap to the radiator. They both jerked back as a geyser of steam shot up from the spout. He waited a moment until it settled down then poured the water in. Sizzling sounds filled the air.

"It's hot, huh?" she said, feeling helpless and out of sorts.

"Yep, it's bone-dry. We'll need some more water."

"I don't have any more."

He turned his head and quirked one brow at her, a quizzical expression that used to make her laugh. But not today. Now she felt nothing but betrayal.

"I thought I taught you to prepare better than that. There's a gallon jug in my truck. Go and get it," he said.

Hackles rose at the back of her neck, but she fought them off. Because she didn't want to argue with him now, she retrieved the jug. Moments later he poured the contents into the radiator. It gurgled as he screwed the cap back on.

"Are you ready for work in the morning?" he asked without looking up.

She snorted. "That depends."

"On what?"

"On whether I can get this old truck to work."

"It'll be working. You'll be there." He sounded positive, as though he expected nothing less.

"Yeah, I hope so."

"As soon as you get into town, take the truck over to Grant Metcalf's garage for a complete overhaul. This piece of junk is overdue," he said.

"It's not a piece of junk," she said.

"Yes, it is." He was too busy tightening bolts and testing the spark plugs to notice her annoyed glare.

"Get in and start it up." Sean stood back, holding a wrench in one tight fist. A streak of grease marred his blunt chin.

She refused to hurry as she climbed into the cab and turned the key. The truck gave a belching growl.

"Give it a little more gas," he called.

She did and the engine roared to life. Sean slammed the hood closed, removed his sunglasses and wiped his damp brow with his forearm. He hopped into the back of the truck, returned Zach's tools to their place then jumped down and leaned against her door.

"You should be okay now, but I'll follow you until we reach your apartment in Minoa." He spoke low, the rich timbre of his voice sending shivers down her spine.

She remembered a time when he would have leaned in and kissed her goodbye. She yearned for him to hold her against her heart again. To tell her that Zach's death was just a bad dream. That he still loved her and everything would be okay. But he didn't. And it did her no good to dwell on the reasons why.

"That won't be necessary. I'll be fine." She didn't

think she could stand to have him on her tail for the next three hours. But in this remote area, there was no help for it. And something about knowing he would be following her tied her insides into knots.

"We're going to the same place, so I'll stay with you until I know you're safe," he insisted.

She bit her tongue, wishing he cared as much about her emotions as he did for her physical well-being.

She gave a bored shrug of her shoulders, thinking she should thank him, but unable to speak the words. "Suit yourself."

"How's your mom?"

She blinked at his sudden question, taken off guard. Over the past decade, he'd shared every Thanksgiving and Christmas dinner with her family. All but the most recent, that is. Her mom had loved him like a second son.

"She misses you," Tessa said.

So do I. But she couldn't understand where that thought came from. She didn't love this man anymore. Not after the way he'd tossed her aside. Her father had done the same thing, and she would never trust another man again.

Sean nodded. "Give her my best."

"Yeah," Tessa said.

A thatch of curly hair fell into his eyes and he brushed it back, his hands covered with grime. A glaze of perspiration shadowed his freshly shaven face and neck and stained the back of his shirt and underarms.

She glanced down at her own shirt. Although she hadn't done much, she'd still managed to get grease on her clothes and hands. Feeling suddenly self-conscious, she reached for a pile of napkins she kept stowed in the door pocket and handed him some. He took her offering and they both rubbed at the stains on their fingers.

Even though she got much dirtier than this when she fought wildfires, the filth bothered her. She told herself it was because she was traveling and didn't want to muck up the interior of Zach's truck. It certainly had nothing to do with her ex-fiancé being here. After all, Sean had seen her many times on the fireline with her face covered in soot. But off the line, she'd always tried to look nice for him. And old habits died hard. Now they were no longer together, it shouldn't matter. And she reminded herself that she no longer cared what he thought.

Sean climbed into his truck and started up the engine. Clicking on his seat belt, he waited for Tessa to pull forward and precede him down the road.

She moved out slowly and he wondered if the trip to Minoa might take all day. Then she picked up the pace, as though testing the strength of her truck.

Correction. Zach's truck. A beat-up old clunker. But the vehicle hadn't always been that way. Sean remembered the day Zach had bought the truck nine years earlier. It had been ten years old at the time, but still in good condition. Sean had donated several hundred dollars to the cause when Zach came up short. Now Sean couldn't help feeling as though the truck was partly his. He and Zach had done a lot of traveling in that vehicle. With Tessa sitting between them like the three musketeers.

Now she resented him. He'd seen that clearly in her beautiful emerald eyes, along with a heavy dose of suspicion. And she had a right. He'd hurt her deeply. Abandoning her, just like her father had done when she was a little girl. It didn't matter that Sean regretted their broken engagement; he wasn't willing to undo it. If he told her of his regrets, she wouldn't believe him. She might even laugh in his face. But he wouldn't put that weapon in her hands. His heart couldn't take it.

Waves of disgust washed over him. A hefty dose of self-loathing followed in its wake. In spite of his breakup with Tessa, he'd made a promise to Zach when she first joined the hotshot crew. A promise he intended to keep. That he'd keep her safe on the fireline. That he'd always look after her and protect her, no matter what.

This was her last firefighting season before she finished her college education. Then she'd move on with her career. Sean had no doubt she'd be promoted fast. Someone as sharp and talented as her would probably become an assistant fire management officer somewhere. In a few years she'd move up to FMO. Once she was working in an office, she'd be safely out of danger. Then he could move on, too. He'd failed to save Zach, but he wouldn't fail again. After this fire season, he'd take a quiet desk job, far away from the trees, smoke and flames. Where he couldn't make any mistakes that might cost someone else their life.

Silently, he yearned for redemption. If only God could forgive him for failing Zach. If only he could forgive himself.

Tessa hadn't mentioned her brother. Maybe they were both too surprised to see each other like this. Out in the middle of nowhere. Taken off guard.

When Sean had seen her sitting on the side of the road, a surge of exhilaration had swept over him. He had his sources. A mutual friend had told him she'd be driving along this deserted road to Minoa today. Though he hadn't planned on coming across her, he'd arranged his own itinerary so that he'd be traveling the same route. Honoring the promise he'd made to Zach, just in case she needed him. And it turned out that she had.

Deep inside, he knew it was more than his promise to Zach that had brought him here today. He tried not to care but couldn't help craving one more glimpse of Tessa's pert, stubborn nose and flawless complexion, one more breath of her long, coconut-scented hair. It wasn't just her beauty that drew him to her, but also her spunk. Her grit. Who she was inside. Something he couldn't explain. A connecting of their spirits.

Nor could he find any respite from the guilt he carried around like a load of bricks in his heart. The psychiatrist he'd visited several times after the fire had said he was suffering from survivor's guilt and PTSD. Because he'd failed to save Zach, he didn't believe he could marry Tessa now. How could he look her in the eye every day of their life together and justify why he'd survived but her brother had died?

She had told him once that she thought there was no justification to ever lose a man or woman's life on a fire. That it always had to be someone's fault. In this case, that someone was him. She must surely blame him. And he'd feared that her doubts and resentment would simmer inside her until they slowly destroyed their marriage. He couldn't put either of them through an ugly divorce. Tessa deserved better than that.

He stared at the back taillights of her trailer. She always packed light. Not a lot of encumbrances to tie her down. That was just one thing he liked about this woman. She didn't require a lot of baggage. But she wasn't happy anymore. He could see that in her wary eyes. And he couldn't blame her. It would take a lot more than eight months for her to trust him again and to recover from Zach's death.

It might take forever.

They stopped in Austin for fuel. Tessa didn't wait for him before she pulled up to a pump, climbed out and started filling her tank. He knew she was very capable, but the gentleman in him forced him to brush her hands aside. She jerked and almost sprayed him with gasoline. The pungent scent of petro filled the air.

"Sorry! But you shouldn't sneak up on a girl." Her face flushed red as a new fire engine.

"I didn't mean to startle you. I just wanted to help."

"There's no need for you to trouble yourself. I can do this," she said.

"I know, but it doesn't sit well with me to let you do this chore when I'm close by." He spoke low and calm, trying not to fluster her. Trying to ignore the tingles of heat shooting up his arm from where their fingers had touched. When they were on the fireline, he had never interceded with her work. But when they were out like this, he felt that filling up her vehicle was the courteous thing to do. Zach had taught him that and so much more.

Inside the convenience store, he bought her a thin piece of jerky and a diet soda. Not because she asked him to, but because he knew they were her favorite traveling foods.

"Thank you." She didn't meet his eyes as she took the items and climbed back into her truck. He got the impression she was purposefully avoiding him, and he thought it was just as well.

Two hours later they pulled into Minoa. Population

three thousand and eighty-four. Including dogs, cats and gophers. The perfect size for a wilderness hotshot crew base.

Tessa drove past Rocklin's Diner, the only restaurant in town, to her small apartment three blocks off Main Street. Her trailer bounced lightly over a speed bump as she pulled into a parking space and killed the engine. She tossed a glance over her shoulder and waved him on, but he didn't go. Knowing she had a trailer filled with heavy boxes to empty before dark, he parked beside her and got out of his truck.

"Now what are you doing?" she asked when she met him at the back of the vehicle.

He flipped the latch on the trailer and pulled the door open wide. "I'm helping you carry your stuff inside."

She bumped him aside with her hip. "Oh, no you're not."

In the past he would have teased her. Tickling her ribs as they jockeyed for position in the trailer. But not now. For two seconds he thought about leaving her alone but couldn't bring himself to do so. Not when she needed him. It just wouldn't be right, even if she was looking at him with a most adorable frown.

Gazing into her eyes, he couldn't help smiling. "You sure look pretty when you're being stubborn."

Her mouth dropped open in surprise. In a rush, he wondered why he'd said such a thing. He had no right to flirt with her. Not anymore. The words had popped out before he could stop them.

To cover up the awkward moment, he reached past her and hefted a beat-up recliner out onto the hot cement. "I thought you had a furnished apartment."

"I do," she said.

"Then why are you keeping this ratty old chair?"

Her gaze lowered to the tattered upholstery and he knew the answer without her saying one word. It had been Zach's chair. She was holding on to anything and everything that had belonged to her brother. Memorializing Zach the only way she knew how.

He almost reached out and brushed a curl off her cheek. Instead, he slid his hands around the armrests. "I miss him, too."

She jerked her head up, her eyes flashing with anger. "Then why did you shut me out? What are you hiding from me?"

He tensed, not knowing how to explain. "I'm not hiding. Let's just drop it, Tess."

"Drop it? Don't you think you at least owe me an explanation?" Her eyes shot him a dart of hostility.

Yes, but he didn't respond, forcing himself to be patient. He'd hurt her deeply and she had every right to be upset. Zach's death had brought him to a standstill. He was haunted by spine-tingling nightmares, recriminations and regrets. But until he figured it out and reconciled it in his mind, he couldn't move forward. But he couldn't go backward, either. In fact, he felt stuck in limbo. And it didn't help that Tessa suspected that Zach's death was his fault.

Her jaw hardened, her eyes spitting flame. For a moment he thought she might chew him out. Instead, she whirled around and reached for a heavy box. Jerking it free of the trailer, she carried it toward the stairs with a stiff stride.

"Too bad you live on the second floor." He grunted as he wrapped his arms around the chair and braced the padded sides against the front of his thighs. Waddling like a duck, he wrestled it over to the bottom of the stairs then heaved it up in a hurried rush.

"It's the one with a view," she called over her shoulder.

At her apartment door, he set the chair down with a *whoof* of air and waited for her to insert the key and open the door.

"Were you planning on moving everything in by yourself?" he asked, knowing she could do it. He'd seen her fight fire, after all. In spite of her fragile features, Tessa was a scrapper. She wasn't overly strong, but she paced herself, using her stamina to work many men under the table.

"I was gonna call Harlie to see if he could help me out," she said.

Hmm. Sean knew he shouldn't mind. Harlie was a member of their hotshot crew and a good man. But the guy was also single and nice-looking. Sean had no right to feel jealous, but he did. A lot. And he wished he didn't.

Within an hour they had the trailer emptied. Sean accepted a drink of water she offered him from the tap in the kitchen. While she busied herself emptying a box, he drained the liquid in three long swallows.

He didn't ask before he went to work helping her put her possessions away. Since she'd spent three summers living in this apartment, he knew exactly where everything went. He stayed in the kitchen, stacking four plates, glasses and pans into the cupboards. He tried not to remember the many meals they'd prepared and shared at the small wooden table, but it all came back like a rushing flood. The decadent desserts Tessa had made. Zach's robust laughter as he teased his baby sister. Sean missed the jubilant camaraderie they'd all enjoyed. They'd been so naive and happy then.

Shaking it off, Sean resumed his work. Within another hour they had everything in order. Tessa set her heavy fire pack beside the front door, ready for work in the morning.

"Do you need anything else?" Standing in the middle of the tiny living room, he gazed at the simple but comfortable surroundings and wished he could stay.

"No, I'm good. Thanks for everything. I appreciate it." She stood nearby, looking up at him with those lovely, magnetic eyes.

He fought off the urge to pull her close against his heart. Every fiber of his being cried out to touch her. To breathe her in. Instead, he slid his hands into his pants pockets and slapped a hard grip on himself. She wasn't his anymore, and he'd better accept that.

"I'll see you tomorrow, then," he said.

She gave one jerking nod and he reached for the doorknob. As he left, he threw a quick glance over his shoulder. She stood right where he'd left her, her eyes mirroring the sadness he felt deep inside.

Chapter Two

The following morning Tessa sat in the training room at the hotshot base with the rest of her twenty-man crew. Leaning her elbows on the desk in front of her, she tried to act interested in what the men were saying but couldn't quite meet that goal. Since all but the superintendent and captain were seasonal employees, they'd been apart all winter long and had a lot to catch up on, but all she could think about was Sean. She hadn't seen him since yesterday. Or Brian, the crew's superintendent, and Rolland, their captain. And she wondered what was delaying their arrival.

"Thanks for the eats, Tessa." Harlie took a big bite out of a chocolate-covered doughnut with pink sprinkles on top. On her way into work that morning, she'd picked up a box of pastries from the local bakery. It was a great morale booster.

The other men added their thanks.

She just smiled and took a sip of her hot chocolate.

"Hey, Tessa. Nice tan. Where have you been all winter? Hawaii?" Dean Clawson waggled his eyebrows at her. As a freshman hotshot, he was new to the squad, and she could already tell he was a big flirt.

She glanced at the man's sandy-blond hair and pale skin. Within a week, she knew he'd be beet-red with sunburn. But by mid-August, he'd be a sun-bronzed firefighter. Women would be flocking to his door. But not her. Since her breakup with Sean, she wasn't interested in dating anyone.

"I've been in Montana. And I'm afraid that bleached body of yours is gonna fry this summer." She spoke deadpan, without blinking.

The men roared with laughter.

"Ouch!" Harlie said.

Their joking was all in good fun, but as the only woman on this crew, she had to hold her own with these macho maniacs, or she wouldn't survive long.

Sean came in from the side office, followed by Jared Marshall, the fire management officer. A tall, athletic man with dark blond hair and dazzling blue eyes, Jared had married Megan Rocklin two months earlier. Megan was the owner of the only restau_ant in town and one of Tessa's best friends. Unfortunately, they hadn't given a lot of notice about their nuptials. Tessa had been in Missoula going to school at the time and regretted that she'd been in the middle of midterms and unable to attend the wedding. But she'd sent the newlyweds an ornate crystal vase and a heartfelt congratulations note.

Hmm. What was the FMO doing here? And where were Brian and Rolland?

"Good morning, and welcome back." Jared waved the group into silence while Sean stood leaning against the wall.

To begin, Jared gave a short, motivational speech

about working as a team and watching each other's backs. He then introduced the two newest members of the crew.

Dean and Ace grinned as they stood and bowed gallantly, undoubtedly showing off to hide their insecurities. Knowing they had a lot to learn, Tessa cheered with the rest of the men. Jared waited for the noise to settle down.

"One last item of business before you start your training. I'm sorry to say that Brian has resigned. He got married in January and moved to Portland last week to be with his new bride."

Pete nudged Harlie with his elbow and smirked as he whispered loudly. "See? I told you so."

A snicker filtered through the men. Tessa would never understand why they found humor in the simplest of things but realized it was merely a pressure valve for the serious work ahead.

"Additionally, you may have heard about Rolland Simpson's wife and eldest daughter being killed in a car crash last week."

A round of gasps and sympathetic sounds came from the group.

"Is Rollo all right?" Harlie asked.

"Yeah, but he's real torn up about it. His youngest daughter survived the crash. Rollo wasn't with his family at the time, but he may not be able to return until the end of the summer fire season. It'll take him some time to get things sorted out. We'll hold his position open for the time being," Jared said.

That meant the leadership of their crew had all but been wiped out. So, who was going to lead the team?

"Sean has been selected as your new superintendent," Jared continued. "I know you'll agree he's highly qualified to be your crew leader and you'll give him the respect due to his position. Since Rollo will be gone for the time being, I'm counting on all of you to help Sean with that extra work."

Tessa's mouth dropped open. She hadn't expected this. No, not at all. Her ears felt clogged, like she was submerged under water. Not in a million years had she thought Sean would be her boss. The leader of the entire hotshot crew.

Hearing the news, Pete sucked in a startled breath. Harlie and Tank's expressions remained stoic. And Tessa knew why. Most of them had been there that fateful day when Zach had died. They weren't sure that Sean was up to this new task. At least, not so soon.

Why hadn't Sean told her about his promotion? Yesterday, in her apartment, he'd had plenty of opportunity. A year ago she would have felt proud and delighted by the news. But right now she couldn't help wondering if he could be trusted to look after the crew's well-being.

The men broke into mild applause, but she could see the doubt in some of their eyes.

Tessa forced herself to clap her hands. She did so with misgivings. After all, Sean had been a squad leader when Zach was killed. But what if he'd been too inattentive, or took an unnecessary risk? It could have been a simple error. One little bad decision that had gotten Zach killed. A tiny bit of information that had been excluded from the incident report. It was one thing to see Sean every day. To work around him and interact. But taking orders from him as he steered the crew through numerous dangerous situations was another matter entirely.

It appeared that she had no choice. Not if she wanted her job.

"Okay, I think that's it. Stay safe out there, take care of each other and fight fire." With a satisfied nod, Jared made his exit to return to the forest supervisor's office.

Tessa didn't say a word as Harlie slid a disc into the overhead projector and Pete switched off the lights so they could watch a training film on how to deploy their new fire shelters. She tried to focus, but her gaze kept wandering over to Sean. Dressed like the rest of the team in a navy blue T-shirt, spruce-green pants and a pair of White's vibram-soled fire boots, he sat on a corner of the desk at the front of the room. He folded his muscular arms, his jaw locked as he stared at the overhead screen.

He turned his head and pinned Tessa with a gaze so intense that she actually squirmed. She looked away quickly, trying to forget what this man had once meant to her. Trying to push aside her doubts over his possible role in Zach's death.

A short time later the crew went outside to exercise. They started with calisthenics and graduated to a three-mile hike up a sharp incline with their forty-five-pound packs on their backs. Tessa stifled a groan and focused on the space right in front of her feet. Good thing she'd kept herself in top physical condition during the winter months or she wouldn't have been able to keep up. She did everything she was asked to do, trying to numb her mind to the arduous months ahead. And when the workday was through, she felt exhausted and as confused as ever.

She was the last of her crew to leave for the day. Darkness covered the earth as she headed outside to her truck. The comforting chirp of crickets came from the cluster of boxwoods edging the length of the garage. She glanced at the gleaming lights of the office. At the last moment she veered off course and headed that way. She didn't know what was driving her, but she had to speak with Sean alone, before she could chicken out. She wanted to find out what he thought about his new assignment. And maybe she might even get him to finally open up and confide in her.

Sean sat at his new desk, his head bowed over a stack of reports and unopened mail. He knew this job well, but with Brian's sudden departure, there was a lot to catch up on.

As he reached for the letter opener, a subtle noise drew his attention. He looked up, a rush of surprise washing over him. Tessa stood leaning against the door-jamb, contemplating him with a slight frown.

"Busy at work, I see," she said.

Was it his imagination, or did her voice sound a bit disapproving? He didn't want any conflict with her right now. Not when he was working so hard to regain the crew's trust. He'd seen the way the men had looked at him after the FMO announced his promotion. The doubt and hesitancy in their eyes. He'd been a member of this crew for years. If this was his last season fighting fire, he was determined to prove himself worthy of the team.

"Do you need something?" He spoke in a brusque tone.

She folded her arms. "Why didn't you tell me?"

"Tell you what?"

"About your new promotion."

He sat back, his chair squeaking. "I only found out myself last night, after I left you."

Which was true. He'd known Brian had eloped and was crazy in love. That his new wife lived in Portland and refused to leave. Which meant Brian had to drive six hundred miles one way every weekend to be with her. It was an impossible endeavor once the hotshot crew got busy with the fire season. Sean had known it was just a matter of time before Brian left the squad and someone else was named superintendent. Until last night, he'd expected that to be Rollo. But making arrangements to bury his wife and eldest daughter and help his younger daughter cope with the loss would take some time, so the captain was out of commission for a while. As one of the crew's two squad leaders, Sean had gotten the job. It had just been one of those things where he was at the right place at the right time for a promotion. But he hadn't known for sure until he'd received the call from Jared.

Tessa tilted her head and peered at him as though seeking the truth in his eyes. "Did you suspect this was going to happen?"

He tightened his jaw. "I don't know much of anything until they tell me. You know how it works."

"How do you feel about this new assignment?" she asked.

"I feel fine. Why do you ask?" And yet he didn't feel fine. There had been a time when he would have loved such a promotion. But now he worried that he wasn't up to the task. He didn't think he could cope if he lost another man, or woman, under his watch.

She dropped her arms to her sides and came to stand in front of his scarred wooden desk. Sean's gaze followed her graceful movements. An old, lingering emotion of attraction filtered through his veins. Why did it have to be this woman who made his heart sing?

"A lot happened last summer," she said.

"And what's that got to do with my promotion?"

She lifted a hand, her face creased with exasperation. "Nothing, I guess."

She obviously didn't trust him. Didn't think he was up to his new assignment. And that bothered him intensely. Because he wanted her to believe in him, even if he no longer believed in himself.

He forced himself to sit very still and not react. But inside, he felt grouchy. He wasn't sleeping well. Always on edge. Crowded rooms made him anxious. His heart raced and his palms got clammy for no apparent reason. The lingering symptoms of PTSD. He still hadn't been able to claw his way out, but he didn't want to tell Tessa that. It was difficult to pretend their breakup wasn't hinged on Zach's death, but Sean knew that was the real cause. He just didn't know how to get past it and make it right.

If only he hadn't taken Zach to work in that chimney area with highly flammable fuels. He'd been Zach's squad leader. He'd talked it over with Zach and they both thought they could get a jump on the fire. The tactic would have succeeded, too, except that squirrely winds had whipped around so fast, they didn't know what was happening until it was too late. The winds brought a buttonhook fire racing uphill toward them. With little time to react, Sean had quickly radioed the rest of the crew to warn them to evacuate. They'd all made it to the safety zone, but Sean and Zach couldn't get there in time. Instead, Sean had tried to take Zach to a previously burned area nearby. It wouldn't be ideal, but they could deploy their fire shelters and ride out the burnover.

Zach wouldn't go. He'd panicked and run the other way. And when Sean had chased after him, Zach had swung his fists so hard that it had knocked Sean down. He'd been dazed as he staggered to his feet. And by the time he'd shaken it off, Zach was gone. Sean thought about going after him, but he knew there wasn't time. Later, Sean was absolved of any wrongdoing, but he still blamed himself. Because he'd been Zach's squad leader. Because he'd chosen life instead of trying to find Zach.

"We're not together now. We don't owe each other any explanations," Sean said.

Tessa lifted her chin, her golden-brown ponytail bouncing against her shoulders. "You mean you don't owe *me* any explanations. Is that it?"

He never could fool Tessa. She recognized his reservations for what they were. A wall. A shield. To keep her and everyone else out. But he couldn't talk about Zach's death right now. He just couldn't.

She leaned forward and rested her hands on top of his cluttered desk. "You almost died in that fire with Zach, yet you act as though it never happened. My brother's death hurt all of us, Sean. It might help if you talk about it."

"With you?" he asked.

"Sure, why not? We were close friends once."

He looked away. They'd been more than friends. She'd meant everything to him. "I know, but the reports have been filed. There's nothing left to say."

"Sure there is. I've tried to give you time. To let you work through this on your own. But it's obvious you're in the same place you were in when I left town last September. Nothing's changed. Nothing's gotten better. I know you're hurting, Sean. But I know there's something you're not telling me."

He stared back at her, forcing himself not to blink. He couldn't tell her about his guilt and PTSD. He had to be strong and overcome it on his own. After all, he was in charge of this hotshot crew now.

"Say something," she insisted.

He grit his teeth. "I have nothing else to say."

He spoke the words low. He heard the doubt in her voice. An edge of suspicion and resentment. His mind told him he'd done everything right that fateful day, but he couldn't believe it. He kept replaying different scenarios over in his mind. If only he'd done this, or that, or something else, then Zach would still be here.

"You used to tell me there was nothing we couldn't do as long as we worked on it together," she said.

A caustic laugh slipped from his throat. "Not this time, Tessa. I'm afraid I was wrong."

She flinched. "If you've given up, then I suppose you're right. We're finished."

A fist of emotion lodged in his chest. He caught a glimpse of pain in her eyes and shook his head.

"What about a medical professional?" she suggested. "There are people trained to help with situations like this. A doctor can help you cope."

That did it. He scooted back his chair and stood, his movements stiff. Reaching for his jacket, he walked to the door and thrust it open. "Look, Tess. I've already visited with a psychiatrist and been cleared for duty. I appreciate this intervention thing you're trying to do here, but I don't need it anymore. I'm fine. Really."

Her lips tightened, her eyes shimmering. Oh, no. Please not that. He could stand anything but her tears.

"I'm just trying to understand. I miss Zach," she whispered.

Ah, that hurt. So much.

"I know you do." He spoke softly, wishing he could do something to make it all better. Wishing he could take away her pain.

"The worst part is that I lost both of you that day. Not just Zach. I lost you, too," she said.

What could he say to that? Nothing.

"I wish things could be different. I wish I could bring him back," he said.

"That's not what I need you to do, Sean. Zach's with God now. But I want to understand what happened and why you have shut me out."

He released a slow breath, trying to ignore the memories of that horrible day as they flashed across his brain. "You've read the incident report. You already know everything."

"Reading that sterile report isn't the same as talking with you, and you know it. I'd rather read your personal notes instead."

"Those are confidential. They're just my ramblings anyway. Nothing you could decipher. The only reason I wrote them down was because my psychiatrist required it." He shrugged, feeling uncomfortable with her questions. He wasn't the type of man to go and visit with a shrink. He'd done it only because he had to.

"I'm Zach's sister. Don't you think I have a right to know the details?" she asked.

"There's nothing left to tell. Unless you want to talk about work, we have nothing to discuss."

She backed up, her face ashen. He'd stung her again, when all he wanted to do was pull her into his arms and keep her safe.

"Fine. If that's the way you want it," she said.

"It is." He tightened his hands, forcing himself not to relent. Not to tell her how he really felt. That it should have been him that died on that mountain, not Zach.

"All right, then. Congratulations on your promotion, Sean. I hope you're happy with your new assignment." She swept past him to the dark parking lot. The tall mercury vapor lights bathed her in an eerie blue glow.

He longed to call her back. To confide in her like he used to. To speak the words he'd kept locked away since that dreadful day. But he couldn't. Not about this. Not without winning her condemnation. Just like the day when he'd broken off their engagement, he let her walk away from him without saying one word to stop her.

When she was inside Zach's truck, he took a deep, settling breath. He watched as she backed out and drove through the front gate, the gravel crackling beneath her tires.

Maybe this fire season wouldn't be as easy as he thought. He had his share of misgivings about accepting this new promotion. He was definitely qualified to lead the team, yet he feared letting them down. What if he couldn't do the job? What if he failed? The thought of losing another man under his command made him sweat, but the thought of losing Tessa absolutely terrorized him. In the past he would have told her his deepest fears. But he couldn't tell her all of this. How could he expect her to understand what he was going through when he didn't understand it himself?

Heaving a labored sigh, he flipped off the lights and

secured the front door. With Brian and Rollo gone, they were down two men. Now the FMO had made him the team's superintendent. A position he had once aspired to. With a college degree in fire science, he had worked hard with the hopes of one day being given his own hot-shot crew to manage. Now that he'd finally reached that goal, he felt deflated. Because it no longer meant anything. Not when he couldn't share the joy with Tessa.

She was angry and hurting, but at least she was safe. She would recover. Eventually. She'd move on with her life and meet some good man who could make her happy. Someone who wasn't responsible for her brother's death. And knowing that she'd share her life with another man hurt Sean most of all. But he had to let her go. Her happiness was more important to him than anything else.

He stood in the empty parking lot, staring at Tessa's taillights as she turned onto the main road. Finally, he drove home. He parked his truck and gazed at his dark house. The black, vacant windows seemed to stare back at him, taunting him with empty disdain. He had to accept that his time of loving Tessa was done and over with. Because he could never have it back.

Chapter Three

Standing in the maintenance room at the hotshot base, Tessa settled into her morning chores with the rest of the crew. They never knew when they might get called out on another fire, so they planned to be ready at a moment's notice.

The whine of the electric belt grinder filled the air in an endless drone. Tugging on a pair of leather gloves, Tessa picked up a Pulaski, removed the tool guard from the steel head and tightened the hickory handle into a bench vise to hold it firm. She reached for a twelve-inch file with a handle and knuckle guard to sharpen the dull edge of the hand tool.

"Hey, Tessa! The Big Guy wants to see you right away." Tank stepped inside the shop and jerked his thumb toward the door.

Tessa tensed. The lighthearted atmosphere frosted over faster than a drop plane could unload retardant on a line of timber. "I'll be there in a few minutes. Tell him to hold his horses."

"Yeah, he said you'd say that." Tank chortled as he turned and left to pass her message along.

"What's up between you and the super?" Dean asked.

A stutter of silence fell over the group. Since Dean and Ace were new to the team, they didn't know her past history with Sean or the doubt they all still felt over Zach's death. What had happened had hurt them deeply, but that wasn't Dean's fault.

Tessa didn't look up, but her heart stopped then pounded like a sledgehammer against her ribs. She had to be careful what she said. Sean was the boss and it wouldn't be good for her to say anything that might undermine his authority.

"What do you mean?" she asked.

Dean shrugged. "I've got eyes in my head. You don't seem to get along very well with him, yet I can tell you both like each other a lot."

"I'll bet they've got the hots for one another," Ace chortled.

Tessa's spine stiffened. In the short time she'd known Ace, she had realized he had a big mouth and a penchant for teasing too much. And right now he was crossing a line with her.

"Mind your own business," she said.

No one else said a word.

"Hey, girl, you don't need to get so testy about it. I was just having fun." Ace blinked and looked away.

Harlie tugged the Pulaski free from Tessa's hands and pushed her gently toward the door.

"I'll finish this for you. Go on and see what the super wants," he said.

She removed her leather gloves and slapped them onto the top of the workbench, half tempted to ignore Sean's summons. She dreaded speaking with him again, especially without the guys present to ease the tension.

Right now she was struggling to concentrate on her work, behave herself and make it through the fire season without getting fired for insubordination.

"I'm going." She stepped toward the door. Her feet felt like chunks of cement, and she paused inside the narrow alcove at the threshold, standing where the men didn't notice her but she could still see them.

Harlie hiked an eyebrow at Ace, his mouth tight with disapproval. "Dude, you're new here, so I'll give you some friendly advice. Don't mess around with something you don't understand."

Ace leaned his elbows on the workbench and cocked one eye. "What do you mean? Can't she take a joke?"

The hackles rose along the back of Tessa's neck and she tightened her hands.

"It's not a joke, man," Chris said. "Tessa and Sean were engaged once, but there's more to it than that."

Dean's eyes narrowed in confusion. "What happened?"

Harlie quickly told the freshman crew members about the wildfire that had swept over them without notice. Hearing the story retold by one of her crew members made Tessa's heart beat like a hydraulic drill.

"We lost communication with home base, but Sean was able to warn us so that we could evacuate the area in time. Everyone got out safe, except for Zach."

"Zach?" Ace said.

"Tessa's brother. He died. The investigation team said it wasn't Sean's fault, but he and Tessa haven't been the same since it happened."

"What do you mean?" Dean asked.

"They broke up."

Hearing the men discussing her relationship with

Sean made her feel irritated and unworthy. Like she'd done something wrong. And she hadn't. Had she? Sean was the one who had taken Zach into that dangerous chimney area to work. And then he'd abandoned her and destroyed their love.

"Do you think it was the super's fault that Zach died?" Dean asked.

Harlie glanced at Pete, their eyes filled with a bit of doubt. Tessa felt their tension. They didn't know what to believe. Neither did she.

"None of us knows what really happened up there," Harlie said. "The super won't talk about it, but he was cleared of any wrongdoing. And that's good enough for me."

Tessa wished she had Harlie's confidence. She wanted to believe in Sean, she really did. But a part of her felt gut-wrenching doubt.

"Does Tessa blame the super for her brother's death?" Ace asked.

Harlie shrugged. "Maybe a little bit. None of us knows for sure. We lost a good man that day, and it's not funny to any of us."

"I'm sorry. I didn't know," Dean said.

"Me either. I didn't mean any harm." Ace bowed his head over a rogue pounder and picked up a screwdriver to tighten the bolts.

Tessa walked out into the sunshine and headed toward the main office. As she passed their buggies, the crew transports they rode in when they traveled to a wildfire, she caught the cloying scent of two-stroke engine fuel. Several of the men were refilling their red sig bottles and Dohlmar containers with fuel.

She glanced at her wristwatch. Almost four o'clock

in the afternoon. One more hour, and she could leave. One more hour, and she'd be home free.

Sean glanced at the stack of incident reports sitting on his desk and tried to concentrate. He picked up a pen and opened the first file, but the letters swam on the page before him. His eyes wouldn't focus; his mind refused to read a single word. For two hours he'd sat there working, pondering what he should do. Tessa wasn't going to like what he had to tell her. He tried to plan a way to break the news to her easily but figured he should just spit it out and be done with it.

The moment she stepped into his office, he knew it without looking up. A blast of air from the swamp cooler in the window carried the light fragrance of her shampoo across the room. Taking a deep inhale, he glanced at the door, his pulse tripping into double-time.

"You wanted to see me?"

She stood in the open threshold, looking as beautiful as ever. Her golden-brown hair had been pulled back in a long ponytail and gleamed against a spray of spring sunlight. A smear of grease marred her chin. Her work clothes were covered in grime, but that didn't diminish the porcelain beauty of her smooth skin. Her alert eyes met his, locking him there. A mixture of pain and hesitation flickered across her face. She looked tired and slightly annoyed.

His chair squeaked as he sat back and gestured for her to join him. "Come on in."

She walked to his desk and slid into a hard-backed chair, her spine stiff, her hands folded primly in her lap. In the past she would have leaned back, crossed her long legs and chatted with him. Her smile had been so easy in those days.

"What's up?" she asked casually, but he caught the throb of emotion in her voice. She didn't want to be anywhere near him, and he couldn't blame her.

"I got a call from Jared Marshall this morning. He's asked us to participate in career day at Minoa High School tomorrow afternoon." There, he'd gotten it all out in one long breath. Short and succinct. No mincing words.

Her eyes narrowed. "Us? You mean the entire crew?"

"No, just you and me."

She exhaled a huff and gripped the armrests with both hands, her fingers whitening. "Can't you get one of the guys to go with you?"

"Sorry, but the FMO wants you and me. He wouldn't negotiate on the issue."

Her lips tightened. "But why me?"

He paused, trying to remember the speech he'd rehearsed numerous times. With her sitting here, the words dropped right out of his brain and he floundered. Tessa had always had that effect on him. The first time he'd seen her, he'd been left speechless for over an hour. "Jared asked specifically for you."

"I still don't understand," Tessa said.

"He believes as the only female on the team, you'll do better to highlight your work as a woman wildfire fighter. As the superintendent of the crew, I'm to accompany you. It's a recruitment trip, but also to build our public relations."

"I'd rather not participate."

Her candor didn't surprise him. From the start he'd

always known just where he stood with Tessa. No pretending. No games. Just pure honesty.

"I understand that, but it'll still be you and me. That's what the FMO wants, and that's what we'll give him." Sean had argued the point with Jared, too, reminding the FMO that things weren't good between him and Tessa. Instead, he'd suggested that Harlie or Tank accompany him. But Jared had been adamant that Sean take Tessa.

No one regretted this last-minute assignment more than Sean. Trotting down to the local high school for career day would provide an opportunity to recruit future firefighters for the crew. For some reason kids on the wrestling team made good firefighters. But going with Tessa was not Sean's idea of fun. He dreaded spending the afternoon with her quiet, questioning eyes.

She hesitated, her spine straightening. He didn't know what he'd do if she refused. A wave of heat flashed over him as he waited for her response. Nerves tingled at the back of his neck. The room seemed to close in on him. A barrage of regrets swamped his mind. More symptoms of PTSD, but he fought them off.

She lifted her shoulders, her forehead crinkled in dismay. "I don't know how to talk to a bunch of teenagers. What am I supposed to say to them?"

"Just tell them what you do. What your days with the crew are like. Tell them about your work as a hotshot. What you had to do to get here. What you do to stay in shape. That kind of stuff."

Her gaze lowered to the papers scattered across his desk and she licked her lips. "I'd rather not go, Sean."

Sean. She'd finally spoken his name again. It had

been so long since she'd said it that hearing it from her lips startled him.

"It'll be okay. You're a natural with kids, Tess. Remember that time when we watched little Brittney while her mom drove her dad to the hospital?" Sean asked.

Brittney was the infant daughter of Tessa's neighbor. The baby's father had sliced his hand on a bread knife and his wife had rushed him to the emergency room in Reno for stitches. Sean and Tessa had spent four enjoyable hours babysitting little Brittney before her mommy came home. It'd been a great evening Sean would never forget, but he wished he hadn't brought it up now. That event seemed so far away. A defining moment that had made him realize he wanted kids. Oodles of them.

She looked away as though his reminder bothered her, too. "Brittney was easy. She was just a baby."

"You'll do fine," Sean insisted.

She shook her head in resignation and Sean felt a sudden chill in the room that had nothing to do with the whoosh from the swamp cooler. Her gaze swept over him, her eyes filled with misgivings. Being near her was a constant reminder of their broken trust.

"Just be yourself and tell the kids about your job. You'll do great," he said with a half smile.

"Okay, fine." She stood and turned toward the door, walking as though the weight of the world rested on her slim shoulders. And he supposed that it did.

He let her go. He longed to call her back. To tell her everything was going to be okay. But things weren't okay, and Sean could never mend the rift between them.

Chapter Four

The following morning Tessa wore her usual navy blue T-shirt with the Minoa Hotshot logo imprinted on the left front side in white lettering. She also wore her matching baseball cap, work boots and spruce-green pants. That was her uniform when she wasn't fighting wildfire.

She'd pulled her long hair into a ponytail that fit perfectly through the hole at the back of the cap. As she walked out into the main yard of the hotshot base, she hoped they'd get called out on a wildfire. Then she wouldn't have to go with Sean to the high school.

It didn't happen.

At one o'clock she climbed into the passenger seat of the supray, the crew's nickname for the superintendent's white pickup truck. Dressed the same as her, Sean waited patiently in the driver's seat while she clicked on her seat belt. Avoiding the bright glint of sunlight through the windshield, she stowed a bag of pamphlets beside her on the seat for their presentation to the kids. They'd briefly talked earlier, just to make sure they'd be in sync with their presentation, but it didn't help a lot.

"All ready?" Sean flashed a smile, his strong hands resting on the steering wheel.

"Yes." She stared out her window, purposefully avoiding his eyes. Being alone with him like this made her feel nervous and jittery. Like she should say something to him, but she didn't know what. Her heart felt too heavy for words and she figured she'd already said enough. Now it was his turn to talk, although she doubted he'd ever address the topic that was weighing so heavily on her mind.

He started the ignition and put the truck in gear. Gravel crackled under the tires as he pulled out of the yard. As he moved into traffic, her tension eased a smidgen. At least they were doing something productive. Something to take her mind off what was really bothering her.

"Remind me again. How many minutes will you want me to take in my presentation?" she asked without looking at him.

"About ten. They asked us to spend twenty minutes total. It shouldn't take long."

Good. A quick in and out. Easy peasy.

"I'm hoping we might be able to recruit some wrestlers for the crew. They're usually strong and in good physical condition," Sean said.

"Yeah, that would be good."

A long pause of silence followed.

"Is your mom still working in the pediatrics office?" he asked.

Tessa blinked, hardly able to believe he was trying to make small talk with her. "No, she retired three months ago."

His brows spiked. "Really? I figured she'd stay working forever. I know she loved her job as a nurse."

"She did, but she's getting older. And losing Zach
changed her priorities. She wants to do something besides work all the time," she said.

Mom's priorities had changed just like Sean's had
changed. Though her mom's changing priorities didn't
include abandoning her.

"What's your mom doing now?" he asked.

"She's taken up painting and wants me to visit soon.
She and Larry are planning a trip to Europe next year.
I told her I'd come home for a short visit after the fire
season is over with."

Larry was her mom's husband, but Tessa had never
considered him her father. The guy was nice enough and
she liked him okay, but she had no desire to get close to
him. Every man she'd ever loved had left her, including
Zach. But Larry took good care of Mom, and that was
all that mattered. The woman had shed enough tears
of grief after Tessa's father had deserted them. Mom
deserved to be happy.

"Soon you'll be back in school. Only one more year
left," Sean said.

She nodded. "Yes."

"And you won't be fighting wildfires after that,
right?"

He sounded almost hopeful. As if he was eager to
have her off the team.

"That's right."

He grunted. "Well, if you need a letter of reference,
let me know. I'll write you a good one."

Remembering the heavy finals she'd completed re-
cently, she released a shallow exhale. She was glad to

be out of school for a little while. "Thanks. I hope all the hard work is worth it when I'm finished."

"It will be. You'll finally reach your goals."

Another long silence, and then Sean gave a low chuckle. "Zach always said you'd get more education than the rest of us, and it looks like he was right."

"I guess so." She remembered how hard her brother had pushed her to get her master's degree. And she thought how easy it was to fall into a quiet camaraderie with Sean. Talking like this almost felt like old times. Almost. And this conversation gave her a glimpse of how they used to be.

"I miss that," he confessed.

"What?"

"Your smile."

She did, too, but she wasn't about to say so. A mountain of caution stood between them like an armored sentinel. Always vigilant, always wary. She longed to make it go away but didn't know how to navigate through her qualms.

"You broke up with me, remember?" She couldn't help reminding him.

His face drained of color and he looked away. "Yeah, I remember."

But he didn't take it back. He didn't say another word.

When they arrived at the school, Sean parked near the red brick building and they went in through a side entrance. A man with a gray mustache and plump cheeks met them in the front office.

"Hello, Mr. Nash. I'm Chuck Garvey, the guidance counselor for the school. Thanks for joining us today."

Sean introduced Tessa and they all shook hands.

"I'm glad you're here," Mr. Garvey said. "We've had two cancellations from our other career specialists this morning. So feel free to take lots of extra time in your presentation."

Tessa's heart sank to the floor. But then she reminded herself that she was a hotshot. If she could fight wildfire, she could talk to a bunch of high school kids with Sean. This was work, and her personal woes had no place here.

"Let me show you to the classroom where you'll be speaking. The students will be arriving shortly." Mr. Garvey led the way down a long hallway that smelled of damp paper towels and pencil shavings.

Inside the classroom Tessa swept past rows of desks and chairs to the front of the room. Several other presenters sat looking expectant, their soft chatter filtering through the air as they spoke politely to one another. Following more introductions, Tessa took a seat beside an accountant and gazed out the wide windows onto the football field. The sprinklers were on, whooshing over the shimmering grass. She made a mental note of the door leading outside and the exercise equipment littering the area near the bleachers. That might come in handy.

A shrill bell rang and Tessa inwardly cringed. As a gawky teenager, she'd never fit in with the other girls her age. She could do without all the primping, gossip and the pressure to dress and act a certain way. Instead, she'd preferred being with Zach and his friends. He'd never seemed to mind.

Within minutes approximately fifteen kids piled into the room, an equal mixture of boys and girls. In a small town this size, Tessa recognized most of them, including Matt Morton. The boy's mom was a widow who waited tables at Rocklin Diner on Main Street. The owner of the restaurant happened to be Megan Marshall, the FMO's new wife. Tessa made a mental note to pay a visit to her good friend as soon as she got some time off from work.

The kids barely glanced at the adults stationed up front, laughing and talking as they found their seats. They slouched in their chairs like they didn't have a care in the world. One student looked up and spotted Tessa. Nudging the boy next to him, he smiled wide.

"Hubba, hubba. This might be fun."

A shrill wolf whistle followed his comment, but Tessa ignored it. She didn't like public speaking, but this wasn't her first rodeo. She had learned to take care of herself in a work environment filled with men. She decided that she could handle a bunch of hormonal adolescents.

Another bell rang and Mr. Garvey stood to give the introductions. Two law enforcement officers would go first, followed by the CPA and then a technology professor from the community college out of Reno. Sean and Tessa were dead last on the agenda.

Hmm. This might take longer than she expected.

Crossing her legs, Tessa put herself on cruise control and waited patiently. She enjoyed the respite, but inside she was quaking. Standing up to speak in front of a bunch of mouthy teenagers made her nervous, especially when she knew Sean would be watching her.

When it was his turn, Sean stood. Ignoring the podium, he walked to the front of the room in his hotshot swagger that said he was in control.

Tessa hid a slight smile.

"Good afternoon," he began, his deep bass voice filling the room like rolling thunder. He sure didn't need a microphone.

"My name is Sean Nash, and I'm the superintendent of the Minoa Interagency Hotshot crew." He gestured toward Tessa, and she stood. "This is Tessa Carpenter, one of my crew members."

A piercing whistle split the air and someone called out from across the room. "Ooo, Tessa. You are fine, lady. Can I work wi' you?"

A round of snickers skittered across the crowd. Simultaneously, Mr. Garvey and Sean jerked their heads in that direction. Mr. Garvey glared and scanned the sea of faces as though trying to pinpoint who had spoken. The group of teenagers stared straight back, looking innocent as newborn babes. Tessa didn't show any reaction whatsoever. But inside she was laughing. She'd been uneasy at first, but now she was in her element.

"Tommie Wheeler, you'll have to ask your mommy about that," Tessa shot back, her face void of expression.

Tommie's gaze widened as though he was surprised that she knew it was him who had spoken. His face flushed red as a new fire engine, his eyes filled with embarrassment.

"Ah-hum! Remember these people are our guests and you will be polite," Mr. Garvey said in a stern voice.

Dead silence fell over the throng. Tommie sat back, his eyes downcast.

Sean gave a scoffing laugh. "I don't blame you for wanting to work with Tessa, but you will have to prove you can keep up with her first. To be a hotshot, you're gonna have to be in prime physical condition."

"I'm a hotshot. I'm prime." A tall boy wearing a letterman jacket flexed the muscle of his arm.

Tessa didn't know the youth, so she held her tongue.

Sean showed a tolerant smile. "Talk is cheap. If you want to be on my crew, you will have to prove yourself." Always quick with a comeback, Sean didn't miss a beat as he answered in a jovial tone, doing an admirable job of keeping things light. Rumbling laughter filled the room as several other boys jostled the athlete. It took several moments for the boys to settle down as Mr. Garvey cleared his throat loudly.

Sean continued his dialogue. "If you were to become a hotshot, some of the things we would train you in are first aid, compass usage, GPS coordinates, chain saws, fire suppression and tactical field work. But first you've got to make the team. I don't accept any complaints or whining, so you better leave that at home with your momma. Attitude is everything in this profession. Members of my crew can hike three miles carrying forty-five pounds on their back in forty-five minutes or less. And you've got to be able to swing a hand tool. All. Day. Long. And sometimes all night, too."

"Without sleep?" someone asked.

Sean nodded. "Without sleep."

"Girls, too?" a female voice called.

Sean nodded. "Girls, too. A crew is only as strong as their weakest member. So the women have to be able to work just as hard as the men and carry their own weight. In addition to that, all crew members need to run one and a half miles in ten and a half minutes or less. You'll do twenty-five push-ups in under one minute, forty sit-ups and at least seven chin-ups. And that's just a few of the physical requirements. There's much more that we'll show you once you're ready to try out for the crew."

A stocky, medium-height boy with a peach fuzz beard gave a barking laugh. Wearing a sleeveless black T-shirt and sporting a skull tattoo on his right arm, he waved a hand in the air. "Ah, gimme something hard to do. That's nothing."

Tessa recognized the boy. His name was Gavin Smith, and she'd heard the stories circulating around town that he was a troublemaker. Drinking, drugs, fighting, painting graffiti and suspicion of theft were just a few of the complaints against the boy. He wasn't good news.

Sean flashed a naughty-but-nice smile at the kid. Lifting his hands to rest on his lean hips, he arched one brow in a skeptical frown.

Oh, no. Tessa knew that look, and it didn't bode well for her, or Gavin.

"What's your name, son?" Sean asked the braggart boy.

"Gavin Smith. What's it to you?" the youth replied with a challenging lift of his head.

Sean wasn't riled by the belligerence in the boy's eyes. He'd heard a few bad things about Gavin. Getting into altercations with the police for suspicion of drugs and vandalism. Arrogant and disrespectful. Sean had been the same way once. And he thought that maybe he could make a difference for the boy. Gavin sat next to Matt Morton, one of the kids from Sean's scouting group, so maybe the two were friends.

"And you think you can do that many push-ups, sit-ups and chin-ups in under a minute each?" Sean asked.

A flicker of doubt flashed across the teenager's face before he gave a hesitant nod. "Yes, I do."

Ah, this was just what Sean was hoping for. He couldn't have planned it better.

"Okay, I'll tell you what. Let's all head outside to that chin-up bar near the bleachers and have a friendly competition. Tessa and you. Let's see who can do the most chin-ups." Sean jutted his jaw toward the window where the exercise equipment sat waiting near the football field.

Out of his peripheral vision, Sean caught Mr. Garvey popping out of his seat, looking flushed and confused. Tessa shifted nervously by his side and Sean sensed that she didn't like this idea, but she didn't say a word.

Turning, Sean met her eyes. "Are you okay with that?"

She hadn't come here to compete, after all. But he'd advised her that he might ask her to show the students a few exercises they could do to get themselves into pristine shape. She'd been warned. Kind of. But he also knew she might get beaten. Women didn't have the upper body strength of men. A strong boy of sixteen or seventeen years might be able to do more chin-ups than she could. Tessa's forte wasn't in her muscular strength but rather in her pacing and endurance. And her determination. In fact, she was relentless.

With a resolute lift of her head, she gazed at the teenager with passive interest. But Sean wasn't fooled. He knew her too well. A spark of fire flashed in her eyes that told him no way was she going to let this snot-nosed kid beat her. Not without putting up a fight. Her gaze didn't waver. Just a lock-jawed resolve that told him the game was on.

"Yes, let's do it." She gave one nod, and that was that.

She didn't say another word and Sean had to hand it to her. In spite of her personal feelings toward him, she was staying professional and aboveboard. And he'd never been prouder of her than at that moment.

"Come on." He waved an arm at the kids and headed for the door.

A mad scramble followed him as he led the way out onto the field. The air smelled of freshly mowed grass. The sun beat down on them like a baking oven, but Sean and Tessa were used to that and more. The students gathered close as he reached into his pocket for his stopwatch.

"Stand back and give our competitors plenty of room," he said.

The kids widened the circle.

Tessa and Gavin faced each other. Sean could see the teenage boy sizing her up. She was shorter by perhaps eight inches and at least forty pounds lighter. When Gavin flashed a confident smile, Sean knew the boy had seriously underestimated his opponent. And then Tessa did something that didn't surprise Sean in the least. Locking gazes with Gavin, she showed a half-crooked smile that spoke volumes. That one expression said it all without saying a word.

You poor sap. You just got had.

Sean quickly organized the event. "We need someone to count each repetition."

Matt Morton stepped forward. "I can do it."

"Good. You stand right here beside the chin-up bar and count out the reps while I run the stopwatch."

With one nod, Matt took his position. Mr. Garvey stood nearby, as well.

"Ladies first." Gavin held out a hand to Tessa.

"Oh, no," Tessa replied in an even tone. "I'm not sentimental. You'll go first."

It was an order, not a question. With that subtle command, Tessa had just taken control of the situation.

Sean almost roared with laughter. He'd seen Tessa do this many times with the other members of the hotshot crew. There was something about knowing how far your competition could go that incentivized you to win. Tessa was strong, but she never beat any of her male crew members on the chin-up bar. But a smart-mouthed teenage boy like Gavin was something different. And Sean was prepared to enjoy this event immensely.

Gavin stepped in front of the bar. He positioned his feet carefully, looked up then down at the ground. He exhaled a giant huff of air. When he glanced over at Sean, he nodded.

"Ready when you are," Sean said.

The boy reached up, gripped the metal bar and began. Sean clicked the watch on, paying close attention to the second hand.

Being young and inexperienced, Gavin pumped hard and fast. At first.

"One, two, three, four..." Matt started to count at a fast clip.

Gavin pulled a bit slower. Sweat broke out on the boy's forehead, and his breathing became labored. One of his hands slipped and he almost fell off the bar. He gave a deep groan, latched on to the bar with a jerk and kept pulling.

"Nine...ten...eleven...!" the crowd counted with Matt.

Gavin slipped again and dropped to the ground, wiping his damp hands on his pants. He was out, but he'd barely made twelve reps. He gasped, red-faced from embarrassment and his exertions. And then he gave a deep hacking cough. Sean knew from the sound that Gavin was a smoker.

"Hooray!" The kids cheered wildly, some of the girls jumping up and down as they clapped their hands.

Matt and several other school jocks wearing letterman jackets pounded the boy on the back. Gavin grinned with victory, but a flash of doubt filled his eyes. He'd fallen before he could finish the repetitions he'd been capable of doing. He'd been too sure of himself and Sean believed it had spelled his doom. Twelve chin-ups in such a short amount of time was impressive, after all. But Sean knew the boy could have done many more. That didn't matter in a competition, nor in wildfire fighting, either.

"Time!" Sean called. "You could have gone on if you hadn't dropped to the ground."

"My hands slipped. They're all sweaty," Gavin grumbled as he swiped them across his T-shirt.

Tessa didn't respond, her face void of expression. Sean knew that, for someone who usually said what was on her mind, she'd learned to keep her feelings to herself in situations like this. Mainly because she knew something that Gavin probably didn't suspect.

Twelve chin-ups was good. Very good. But the larger a person was, the harder the reps became because they had more body weight to pull up.

Because of the calories she burned on the job, Tessa didn't weigh more than a hundred and ten pounds soaking wet. She regularly pulled between thirteen and fifteen chin-ups every day during their exercise regimen. Not because she had to, but because she pushed herself hard at everything she did. To keep herself in prime physical condition to fight fire with the men.

Wiping her hands against her pants to remove the dampness, she then rubbed them in the dirt to make sure her palms were good and dry. Reaching up, she gripped the bar and began. Moving at a steady pace, she bent her knees slightly. As she found her rhythm, she used her legs like a frog, pumping them in the air to help propel her upward as she pulled with her arms. She used her entire body, moving in an easy, steady rhythm, so she wouldn't burn herself out before she met her goal. She'd done this so many times, she knew it by heart. And watching the clock became difficult for Sean. He wanted to watch her. He could hardly take his eyes off her graceful motions.

"Twelve...thirteen...fourteen!"

Both Gavin and Matt groaned in defeat. Some kids were more generous, especially the girls. Even if Tessa was the opponent, they got caught up in the moment and counted out her reps.

"Eighteen...nineteen...twenty!"

"Time!" Sean called.

Tessa dropped to the ground, her breathing coming fast and hard. She'd reached a new record for herself. Watching her, Sean realized she'd worked hard but knew what to expect and how to get the most out of her body. No bending over and heaving and blowing for her. No, sirree. And Sean knew it was because she saw that as a sign of weakness. And there was very little weakness in this woman.

Gavin stared at her, openmouthed. "Hey! How did you do that?"

She smiled a knowing smile then reached out and

clapped the boy's shoulder. "Why don't you come down and visit our hotshot base in the next week or two and I'll tell you how. We could use a good man like you on the crew next summer, if you're interested in fighting with the best. We can tell you how to get yourself in shape and put you through the training requirements. But you'd better give up the cigarettes first. They ruin your lungs and cause a lot of other health problems."

Sean almost swallowed his tongue. She'd said verbatim what he'd planned to say to Gavin. Sean recognized raw talent when he saw it. Gavin might be a bit wild and rough around the edges, but they'd teach him, if he'd listen. If he would train and work hard. If the kid was willing, they could pull him out of his wild lifestyle and set him on the road to something beneficial and productive.

Gavin flashed a smile. "Maybe."

His answer meant *no*, but Sean wasn't deterred. He intended to help this boy, if he could. If Gavin would let him. The way that Zach and Tessa had once helped him.

While Tessa faced the crowd, Sean handed Gavin a pamphlet with his name and phone number written at the bottom. He hoped the boy would call soon. If not, Sean would follow up with Matt and enlist some help.

"You want to know what I do as a woman wildfire fighter?" Tessa spoke to the group in a loud, confident voice. "Well, I'll tell you. I fight fire. Right alongside the men. I get just as dirty and work just as hard as they do. Don't you girls believe it when someone says you can't do what the guys can do. Most women aren't as strong as a man, but there are other ways for us to compensate. Learn to pace yourself. Learn patience. And if you're interested in becoming a hotshot, give us a call. If you're willing to work hard, I'd be happy to help you along."

Several tendrils of golden-brown hair framed Tessa's face and were slightly damp from her exertions. In spite of what she'd just done, she looked feminine and pretty. She brushed the hair aside and reached for the bag she'd brought and started handing out pamphlets. Kids crowded around her, including several girls. A heavy dose of respect gleamed in their eyes. Tessa laughed and joked with them, answering their questions.

Watching her work, Sean stood back and folded his arms. He couldn't suppress a burgeoning pride that welled within his chest. And to think she'd been nervous about talking to these teenagers. All he could think at that moment was what a remarkable woman she was.

His woman. Or at least, she used to be. And knowing that he'd lost her punctured his heart. But he had no one to blame but himself.

"That was amazing." Mr. Garvey stood beside Sean and grinned. "We've never had such a successful career day. I've never seen the kids this enthused before."

Sean nodded. "Good. I'm glad we could help. And thank you for inviting us. We appreciate it, too. I suspect we'll get one or two good firefighters out of this group."

Minutes passed as Sean and Tessa mingled with the students. By the time they finished their work, packed up and headed back to the hotshot base, all Sean could think was how right the FMO had been to send them together to this event. But their work was as far as being together would ever go.

Chapter Five

The moon shone bright and round in the evening sky when Tessa and the rest of the crew finally got off work that night. She loved the longer days of summer, but it also meant extended work hours. On the hotshot crew, they didn't quit until the work was done. If they had equipment to clean and sharpen, or other special tasks to do, they kept at it until it was finished.

She parked her truck along the sidewalk edging Rocklin Diner. As she got out and headed for the door, her stomach rumbled. A single streetlight cast an eerie gleam over the sidewalk.

The bell above the door to the restaurant tinkled gaily as Tessa stepped inside. All at once, she was engulfed by the tantalizing aromas of fried chicken and apple pie. Still wearing her dusty hotshot uniform, she glanced around, noticing the place was almost empty. Not surprising at this late hour. Most people had already had their supper and gone home.

Harlie and Dean sat in a corner booth, their faces still covered in grime but their hands freshly washed.

"Hey, Tessa! Come and join us." They waved her over.

"Thanks, guys, but I want to talk to Megan for a while." She smiled and pointed as she slid onto a tall stool at the front counter.

The diner was a regular meeting place for the hotshots, but Tessa wanted to be alone right now. The guys smiled, seeming to understand.

"Hi, Tessa." Megan Rocklin waved to her from behind the salad bar.

Correction. Her name wasn't Rocklin anymore. Not now that she was married to Jared Marshall, the fire management officer.

In spite of being the owner of the place, Megan wore blue jeans and a short apron with straws and a notepad sticking out of the front pocket.

Tessa hugged her good friend. "It's so nice to see you. Marriage suits you."

"It's good to see you, too. You look so great."

As Tessa leaned her elbows on the clean counter, she glanced at her grimy clothes. "Yeah, right."

Megan chuckled and slid a menu in front of her. "Sean kept you hotshots late at work tonight."

Tessa nodded, not opening the menu. "Yes, we were clearing a new trail in the park and I'm famished. What's the special this evening?"

"Chicken fried steak. The grill's still on, so we can make whatever you like."

"The special sounds good," Tessa said. "With mashed potatoes?"

"Of course." Megan quickly jotted some notes on her pad and snapped the order up for the cook. Then, knowing what Tessa liked, Megan got her a glass of milk and a glass of ice water.

"How are you doing?" Megan asked as she slid the beverages onto the counter.

Tessa didn't pretend not to understand. Before she'd married Jared, Megan's first husband had been a member of the crew and was killed in the line of duty two years earlier. The two women had been friends for several years, but the fact that Tessa had lost her elder brother in a similar situation last summer gave them something in common.

"I'm fine, all things considered."

Megan paused, a heaviness filling her voice. "How is work going this season?"

"It's okay."

Megan leaned closer and spoke in a lower voice, so the other hotshots wouldn't overhear. "You don't sound so certain. How is it between you and Sean?"

Tessa released a heavy sigh. Like everyone else in town, Megan knew about Tessa's broken engagement. "I do my work and try to avoid him."

Megan gave a sad little laugh. "I know it can't be easy between the two of you right now."

"We just do our jobs." In the past Tessa would have opened up and confided more to Megan. But now the woman was married to the FMO, Tessa's big boss, and she didn't want confidential things getting back to him. It wouldn't be good form. He might tell Sean. Or he might take it all wrong and decide that she shouldn't be working on the crew anymore. And none of those outcomes pleased Tessa.

"It's Zach's birthday on Sunday," Tessa said.

Megan rested a hand on top of a napkin dispenser. "Are you going to visit him at the cemetery?"

"Yes, right after church." And Tessa realized maybe

that was why she was feeling his loss a bit more deeply than usual. Thinking about her brother made her throat constrict.

"Tell him I miss him, too, will you?" Megan said.

"Of course." Tears burned Tessa's eyes, but she blinked them back. It didn't matter. Megan wasn't fooled and handed her a clean tissue.

"I didn't think Sean would be coming back this year," Tessa said.

Megan tilted her head. "You mean here to Minoa? On the hotshot crew?"

"Yes. I was stunned that he was named the new superintendent, too." Tessa didn't need to explain about Brian's recent marriage and resignation, or Rollo's sad family situation. No doubt Megan already knew.

"I must admit, I was also surprised that Sean remained in town after all you two went through. I also thought he would leave the area," Megan admitted.

"Apparently he decided to stay."

"Any idea why?" Megan asked.

"No. Conversation with him is like talking to a brick wall."

"How's he doing? I mean, really. How is he? And you know what you tell me will remain between us. I won't tell Jared a thing."

Tessa wiped her nose. Based on their past relationship, she trusted Megan to keep a confidence, even from Jared. But an innocent slip of the tongue could divulge private information to the FMO. Tessa didn't want to cause any more problems, nor did she want to put Megan in a position where she would have to watch what she said around her own husband.

"Honestly, I don't know how Sean is, but I can tell you that he's still a stubborn mule," Tessa said.

Megan laughed. "Yes, but that's one of the qualities that makes him a great firefighter. I just wish you two could get back together."

"No. He doesn't love me anymore, Megan."

"Did he say that?"

"In so many words. He said he didn't want me anymore, that he wanted something else. So I took that to mean he doesn't love me."

"Do you still love him?"

Tessa hesitated, searching her heart. But all she felt was a numbing ache. "No, not anymore."

A niggling doubt caused her to look away. Sean had broken her heart, and it had crowded out all the love she'd once had for him. Now she could barely stand to be in the same room with the man.

Megan retrieved a platter of salt and pepper shakers from beneath the counter and started refilling them. "I find that hard to believe. A love like what you two shared doesn't die easily."

Tessa snorted. "It has for Sean."

"I don't believe that," Megan said.

"It's true. He's not the same now. He's changed and we've both moved on."

Or had they? Of course they had. So why couldn't she stop thinking about him? Or feeling like they still had unfinished business between them?

"I'm sorry to hear that. I truly understand how you feel. The loss. The grieving. They seem to go on forever. I wish there was a way to go back in time and undo everything," Megan said.

"Me, too," Tessa said.

But it wouldn't bring Zach back. And Tessa knew her breakup with Sean was for the best. He could be hiding something from her. She might never know what really happened to her brother. And she could never marry a man she didn't trust. Nor could she marry a man who wouldn't open up and talk to her about difficult issues. She wanted to be a team with her husband. To have a marriage where his hurt was her hurt, his pain was her pain, his victory her victory and his concerns her concerns. To have oneness of heart and mind. And that wasn't possible with Sean right now.

Megan made a tsking sound. "It must have been terrible for Sean. Battling the flames and fighting for his life. It's a dangerous profession. Why should we be surprised when someone we love gets killed doing it?"

Tessa met the other woman's eyes. "How did you get over losing your husband?"

Megan showed a sad smile. "I'll let you know if it ever happens. But for now I can tell you this. After Blaine died, I promised myself I'd never love another firefighter as long as I lived."

"Really?" That was amazing news, considering Jared Marshall was the fire management officer. And before that, he'd been the superintendent of a hotshot crew, just like Sean. As the FMO, Jared wouldn't be on the front lines fighting the flames, but he'd always be involved in firefighting to some degree.

"Yes, really. When I met Jared, I fought my feelings toward him for a long time, but then I had to give in. Sometimes our heart knows what's best for us. We don't always get to pick who we fall in love with. It just happens to us. And then we have to turn the rest over to the Lord. We have to trust Him to take care of the ones we love."

Tessa nodded, understanding completely. But it was much easier said than done. She'd always had a strong faith in God, and she'd tried to hand her anger and hurt over to Him. But her doubts still niggled at her. Maybe they always would.

"How did you learn to trust in love again?" Tessa asked.

"My faith in God helped a lot. I learned to rely on Him. I'm guessing Sean is suffering from survivor's guilt. He's probably wondering why he lived when Zach died. It must be so difficult. Trying to understand. Trying to cope with what happened. And wondering if there was something he could have done to save Zach."

Tessa chewed her bottom lip, fighting off a sense of compassion for Sean. A part of her still blamed him for Zach's death. If he hadn't taken her brother into that chimney area to work, then Zach might still be alive.

"I just wish Sean would talk to me about it. I wish he'd help me understand what happened," Tessa said.

"It wouldn't change anything if he did. Zach's gone and you can't bring him back," Megan said.

But it might dispel Tessa's doubts. It might restore her faith in Sean.

Megan reached out and clasped Tessa's hand in hers. "Look, sweetie. Can I give you a bit of loving advice?"

Tessa nodded, knowing Megan had her best interests at heart.

"Be patient with Sean. He'll come around. Just don't give up on him. You both need time to grieve and sort this out. Trust him," Megan said.

Not likely. Not anymore. In fact, Tessa doubted she'd

ever love another man again. Men had brought her nothing but heartache.

She reached for her glass of ice water and took a long swallow. She appreciated Megan's friendship more than she could say. It felt so good to confide in someone. If she didn't have to work with Sean every day, she wouldn't care if she never saw him again. She'd already given up on him.

She released a heavy sigh, remembering that horrible day when Zach had died. The heavy smoke. The scorching heat. The crushing fear when she'd been told that both her brother and Sean were missing.

Megan and her two young children had been coming down off the mountain after delivering food supplies to the fire camp. They were caught in the same fire. Jared had found Megan and her kids just in time and they took refuge in Gosser's Creek. Otherwise, they might have died, too.

"Do you think Sean did something to cause Zach's death?" Tessa asked.

"No. Honey, they would never have promoted Sean if he'd done something wrong. That's the way it works," Megan said.

The woman sounded so certain. She had so much faith in Jared's judgment. Tessa wished she could have that kind of confidence in Sean. She knew he was a favorite with the Forest Service administration. He was a workhorse who got results. No wonder they'd promoted him. She just hoped he wasn't hiding something they'd overlooked. Something even they didn't suspect. She didn't believe Sean would have knowingly put Zach at risk, but negligence was just as deadly. He might have been careless or inattentive, and she would never know unless he told her. And maybe that was why he refused to talk about it. She had no way of knowing for certain.

A bell rang and Tessa jerked. Megan turned and reached for a plate of food the fry cook had just set beneath the warming lamps. She slid the plate in front of Tessa and smiled.

"Eat up. And be of good cheer. It'll all work out for the best," Megan said.

Tessa hoped so. She picked up her fork, trying to focus on her food. She caught the tantalizing aroma, but somehow she wasn't hungry anymore. She forced herself to take a bite and wondered again why Sean had stayed on the crew. He had a lot of wildfire experience and would be an asset working on any forest in the nation. He didn't need to stay in sleepy Minoa, Nevada. So why had he changed his mind and remained here?

"Just trust God and follow your heart," Megan said as she stepped away from the counter.

Follow her heart. She had no idea what that was anymore. Nor did she have any desire to mend her relationship with Sean.

The bell above the door tinkled as a man walked into the restaurant. He sat at the opposite end of the counter and nodded expectantly. With one last understanding smile, Megan went to serve him.

Tessa barely tasted the tender meat and potatoes. Her thoughts were tied up in her conversation with Megan. And when she finished her meal, Tessa stepped over to the cash register to pay her bill. She chatted a few more minutes with Megan. General stuff about the woman's two sweet kids that had nothing to do with what was really troubling her. And when Tessa stepped outside into the cool night air, she had a lot to think about.

* * *

Sean slowed his truck and turned off the main road at the edge of town. Two more blocks, and he pulled through the tall arches at the opening of the cemetery. A wrought-iron fence circled the perimeter. Headstones dotted the wide-open field, which was segmented by narrow dirt roads. The sprinkler system whooshed over one section of lawn on the west side. Through the open window of his vehicle, Sean caught the earthy scent of freshly mowed grass.

He parked on the east side, beneath a thick stand of aspens that edged the lane. Reaching across the seat for the bouquet of lilies he'd picked up at the florist shop, he opened the door and got out. Stepping past the sheltering trees, he looked up and stopped dead. His heart thudded and he felt a moment of panic blaze through him.

Tessa was there. Wearing a flower-print dress and strappy high heels, she knelt before Zach's grave, her head bowed low. She gazed at her brother's headstone, one hand pressed against her lips. As though she was speaking privately to her brother, or crying.

Maybe both.

It was Sunday and Sean figured Tessa had been to church. In the past he would have accompanied her. Wearing his best dress suit, a white Oxford shirt and tie. Delighting in the feel of her hand resting on his arm as they sat in the chapel and worshipped God. He'd never been much of a praying man, but that had changed when he met Tessa. After they'd started dating, he'd developed a fledgling faith. His love for Tessa and his belief in God had made him want to be a better man.

But Sean couldn't bring himself to go to church anymore. Not with all the black, ugly feelings coursing through his heart and mind. He figured he'd be struck by lightning if he entered the Lord's house. He didn't feel worthy anymore. And frankly, it'd been a year since he'd prayed. He just couldn't talk to God after what had happened.

Now Sean didn't want to intrude on Tessa's private time. He took a step back the way he'd come, planning to get in his truck and leave. But she glanced up and saw him there.

Sean froze.

Her mouth dropped open in surprise. She brushed her hands across her eyes. Now that she'd seen him, it'd be rude to flee. He'd never been a coward before, but now he was. He didn't know how to comfort her loss.

Pinning him with her gaze, she stood and dusted leaves and twigs off her bare knees. She wore her long, golden-brown hair in a mass of soft curls around her shoulders, warm and inviting. Her dangly earrings glittered in the bright sunlight. If he hadn't seen her fight wildfire, he would have thought she was a complete girly-girl. And that was just one more thing he liked about this woman. She was an enigma. Two contrasting pieces of a very complex puzzle. Strong and gutsy, yet completely feminine and vulnerable.

Pushing a stray curl back from her cheek, she didn't wave. She just stood there, a slight frown pulling at her brow.

Taking a deep breath to settle his nerves, he walked to her. As he got closer, his heart beat madly in his chest.

"What are you doing here?" she asked. Her mascara was smudged just enough to give her an alluring smoky-eye look.

"I came to visit Zach." The green tissue paper around the lilies crackled as he tightened his fingers over the long stems.

Her gaze lowered to the delicate flower petals and her eyes widened. "You brought him flowers?"

Her voice cracked and so did his heart. He nodded, his throat tight with tender words he longed to say to her. A feeling of compassion welled up inside him, but he couldn't comfort her. Not without misleading her into thinking he wanted to get back together.

She gave a sad little laugh. "So, you're the one who's been leaving lilies on Zach's grave every week. I noticed them before I left town last summer and then again for the couple of weeks since I've been back."

He gave a noncommittal shrug. "Not every week. Sometimes I'm too busy to make it over here."

"Oh." Her eyes rounded as the realization dawned on her.

He hadn't meant for her to find out. The flowers were a simple way for him to remember a dear friend.

"He'd like that," Tessa said.

Sean shrugged. "He wasn't big on flowers, but it seemed fitting."

"I miss him."

"Me, too," he confessed and immediately regretted it. Because it paved the way for more discussion, and he didn't want that now. Not with Tessa. All he wanted to do was hide from her wounded, accusing eyes.

"What do you miss the most about him?" she asked.

"Tess, I've got to get going."

"No, I'd really like to know," she said.

He took a deep inhale, sensing she needed to talk about her brother. Sean did, too, but he didn't want to give her the wrong ideas.

He heaved a sigh of resignation. "I miss his friendship and wise advice."

She quirked her brows. "Really? I always thought Zach was a comedian, not an adviser."

"Not with me."

"What did he advise you about?" she asked.

"Whenever I had issues with my squad, I asked him what I should do. He always knew what was right. And sometimes, he'd give me advice about you."

Her brows spiked. "What about me?"

"Oh, just little things."

She took a step closer. "Such as?"

"He said you love pink roses, but you don't care for lilies because they remind you of funerals. And he's the one who told me your favorite date is pizza and a movie at home." He glanced at the flowers he'd brought for Zach, wishing he'd chosen something else today.

She laughed. "So, that's why you brought me pink roses and we stayed at home and ate pizza for our first date."

"Yes, that's why."

"It's amazing that the two of you knew that about me. But I thought Zach always went to you for advice, not the other way around."

"He came to me occasionally. I always knew I could count on him whenever I needed help. Next to you, he was my best friend in the world."

Okay, so much for not confiding in her. He figured he'd just thrown the gate wide open with that last comment.

"You have a funny way of showing it," she said.

He tilted his head. "What do you mean?"

"Best friends don't abandon each other."

Was she referring to Zach, or the way he'd abandoned her?

He nodded and looked down, feeling her censure. "Yes, you're right. I wish I could have stayed with Zach."

"From what I understand, you would have died if you had stayed with him. They found his body down by the creek, but you were up in a previously burned area. You must have gotten separated in the firestorm."

He took a deep inhale then let it go. "Yeah, something like that. Can we talk about something else?"

She pursed her lips. "Sure, what would you rather talk about?"

"Anything, I guess. I just… I just can't talk about Zach right now."

"I understand, but he was my brother, Sean. I don't want to forget about him. He was so good to me. He was the glue that kept Mom and me going after my father left. He became the patriarch of our family. Now that he's gone, can't we remember him with fondness?"

"Of course."

Sean didn't know what else to say. He'd been in her life for so long now that he thought he knew everything about her, including her relationship with Zach. But he was wrong. She continued to surprise him over and over again.

She contemplated the pretty white flowers. "I actually love lilies now."

"You do?"

"Yes, because they're the flower of the resurrection. And they remind me that I'll get to see Zach again one day. Because of Christ's atonement, there is no ending."

He nodded. "That's nice. I like that."

"Whenever you and Zach were together, you always made me smile," she said.

"When the three of us were together, it was fun. He loved you very much," he said.

"I know he did."

He felt the need to reassure her, but he didn't dare tell her about his vow to keep her safe. She'd probably be furious about that. So he had become her silent protector.

They both were quiet for a time, lost in their own thoughts. Her pale skin glowed in the sunlight, but her eyes were clouded.

"Why did you take him into that chimney area to work?" she asked quietly.

He blinked, feeling as though she'd just slugged him in the gut. The quiet moment between them seemed to pop like a delicate bubble. "It was a good idea at the time. We both thought we could get a jump on the fire. We didn't know it would turn out bad, Tessa."

"Well, it did." She stepped back, breaking the moment. "I'd better get going. Mom will be calling me later this afternoon and I don't want to miss her."

"Yeah, sure."

The air between them seemed to frost over with tension. His throat tightened. In spite of losing her dad and now Zach, she still had a family who loved her. And he'd cherished the idea of becoming a part of that with her.

He could never forget growing up in foster care. The loneliness. The feeling of being unwanted. Like he was a burden. No one to depend upon. No one to watch his back. But that had changed when Zach had introduced him to Tessa. He'd had her and her family to belong to. For a little while. But now he knew if he talked about what happened with Zach, she'd never be able to forgive him. She would blame him. She probably already did. Just like he blamed himself.

He backed away, thinking he never should have come here. Never should have stayed in Minoa. The moment he'd seen her standing in the cemetery, he should have walked away.

He noticed that she'd wiped the dust and leaves off the chiseled stone marking Zach's grave. Her eyes shimmered. She coughed as though she had something stuck in her throat.

"I'll see you at work tomorrow," he said.

"Uh-huh, tomorrow."

She walked away to where she'd parked Zach's truck on the west side, partially obscured behind the gardener's hut. No wonder he hadn't seen her and known she was here. Otherwise, he wouldn't have stopped.

He sensed that something had shifted between them. For the first time in a long time, they'd talked about Zach. Good memories. Sean knew he hadn't given her the answers she sought, but it was a start that might help her heal a little bit.

As he watched her drive away, a riot of emotions clambered inside his head. He wanted to run after her. To say something to make it all better. But he couldn't.

He felt heavy as though an anchor were tied to his chest and pulling him down to the ground. He must not get emotionally attached to Tessa again. Loving her would only break his heart over and over, because he couldn't bring Zach back. Nothing could mend this rift between them. Not ever.

Chapter Six

"Fire! Fire!"

Tessa snapped her head up and stared at Sean's white frame house. Standing on the sidewalk bordering his immaculate green lawn, she had just parked her truck along the curb. Late-afternoon sunlight glinted off his black mailbox. Carrying a file of inventory reports beneath one arm, she had initially headed toward his front door. She'd rather not have come here, but Sean had said it couldn't wait until tomorrow. No big deal. She'd drop off the reports and leave. In and out.

"Fire! Help!" someone yelled again from the back-yard. The cry was followed by a round of male laughter.

Tessa gripped the manila folder in her hand as she changed course and sprinted across the grass. She hurdled a flower bed filled with pink and purple petunias. Having been here zillions of times before, she knew the way with unerring accuracy.

At the patio, she came up short and peered through the shade of several tall wisteria trees.

"This isn't a laughing matter, boys. Try to take it seriously."

Owen Larson, a man Tessa recognized from the town's volunteer fire department, stood beside four teenage boys. Three of the kids were dressed in Boy Scout uniforms. The fourth boy was Gavin Smith, whom she'd beaten in the chin-up competition at the high school a week earlier. In spite of the yelled warnings she'd heard, the group didn't seem panicked. In fact, the boys snickered and jostled one another as though they were having fun.

Sean stood with his back to her. She stared at him, stunned to the tips of her toes. When had he gotten involved with the Boy Scouts? She was used to seeing him in his hotshot uniform, but this was something entirely different. He looked so strong and yet so vulnerable. All she could figure was that he was doing a training exercise for future hotshot recruits. But these boys seemed kind of young, not one of them over the age of seventeen. It'd be at least a couple of years before they could qualify for the crew.

The teenagers were unaware of her presence as they milled around the open fire pit. In a town this small, she wasn't surprised that she knew almost all the boys here. Gavin Smith, Matt Morton, Derek Wilson and Teddy Gardner. Local boys whose folks gathered at church with Tessa every Sunday.

Gavin stood out like a broken thumb, his long chestnut hair falling carelessly over his high forehead. His black sleeveless T-shirt seemed so stark against the skull tattoo on his right arm. Tessa knew that he lived with his grandfather, a kind old gentleman who had stepped in several years ago when Gavin's father had died of a drug overdose and his mom had left town with another man. No wonder Gavin seemed so lost.

With all the other boys dressed in starched uniforms, he looked like he didn't quite belong. And the thought flashed through Tessa's mind that maybe the other boys would have a positive influence on him. He obviously needed a good friend.

A card table sat nearby. On its top rested a pile of books and papers, a box of kitchen matches, a smoke alarm and a red fire extinguisher.

"Come on, Matt. You know what to do." Sean stood off to the side, not yet aware of Tessa's presence.

Matt scrambled for the extinguisher, knocking a tripod and easel askew in the process. A large poster bumped against the table and clattered to the ground. The boy hesitated, his eyes filled with frustration as his face flushed with embarrassment. He paused to pick up the mess.

"No, Matt. Keep on going," Sean encouraged. "The fire is the most important thing right now. You can clean up everything after the fire is out."

Sean stood with his legs slightly spread, his strong hands on his lean hips. Tessa recognized his *hotshot-superintendent-I'm-in-charge* stance, and she hid a smile of amusement.

Matt snatched up the extinguisher, pulled the ring, lifted the discharge nozzle and sprayed the fire pit with a deluge of water. No foam. No fire retardant. Just water. Sean had used this special extinguisher before, when he didn't want to clean up the sloppy spray of retardant all over the place.

Owen stepped back just in time, but the other kids got soaked in the process. They yelled and jumped out of the way as they each took almost a direct hit from the nozzle.

"Hey! You got me all wet," Gavin yelled.

"Me, too." Teddy glared his disapproval as he wiped his damp Boy Scout shirt.

Sean laughed. "That'll teach you to get out of the way next time."

Owen merely shook his head. "Just be grateful it wasn't foam. The water will dry off soon enough."

In response, Matt aimed the extinguisher at Owen and Sean and let her rip. The two men gasped as the water struck them square in the chests. They yelled and chased the boy around the yard. Loud laughter rang through the air as the other boys joined in, chasing and spraying one another with squirt guns. By the time they settled down, each of their Scout uniforms was soaked.

Sean laughed, the sound deep and mellow. Watching him interact with these kids and hearing the rich timbre of his voice did something to Tessa. It rushed over her like a soothing balm to her tattered heart. It sounded so good. So happy and normal. She could almost forget her troubles.

"Good job, Matt. You not only put out the fire, but you also cooled everyone off." Sean smiled wide as he clapped the boy on the shoulder and reached to take the now-empty fire extinguisher.

Matt grinned from ear to ear, looking utterly delighted with himself. He handed the extinguisher over like it was a dangerous weapon. As he did so, he noticed Tessa and jutted his chin toward her. "Hey! We've got company."

Sean turned, his eyes widening at the sight of her. The boys instantly quieted down, their laughter and raucous voices fading. They stared at her like she had a third eye stapled to her forehead.

"Tessa. I didn't know you were here." Sean glanced down at his own damp Scout uniform. The fabric molded to every bulge of his muscular chest and arms.

And that was when she saw the scars on his left arm. At the hotshot base, he usually wore a long-sleeved T-shirt. But not today. His short sleeves revealed long, ugly welts covering his forearm. And she knew where they had come from. He'd received some severe burns during the fire that took Zach's life.

"Ooh, Sean's got a girlfriend," Matt teased.

"Hey! Be polite." Owen slipped an arm around the boy and gave him a noogie on his head. The two tussled for several moments, drawing the other boys' attention. They all ended up in another wrestling match.

Didn't these boys take anything seriously? While they scuffled around, Sean met her eyes.

"You got the report finished quickly. I expected you later," he said.

She slid her free hand into her pants pocket, feeling out of place. "Um, I had most of it already up-to-date. I just needed to check a few things to make sure my report was accurate and I thought I'd bring it right over."

"Great. Can you give me just a few minutes to finish up here?" He indicated the boys.

"Sure." She stood back, hating the tense politeness between them. So much for her goal to stay as far away from him as possible. At this rate, it was going to be a long summer.

"Okay, gather around," he called.

The group did as asked, their boisterous sounds dying down. Tessa listened with curiosity.

"You all did a great job today," Sean said. "I think you'll be ready to help with the Community Cleanup

Project next week. But don't forget the fire tetrahedron. If you've got a fire, what are the three elements you want to deprive it of?"

"Oxygen, heat and fuel." The boys shouted the words simultaneously. With each response, Sean counted it off until he held up three fingers.

"Good! Now line up and Owen will sign you off on what you learned today. And don't forget we'll be meeting here again the same time next Tuesday to finish up the fire safety merit badge. Unless I'm called out on a fire, that is. If that happens, Owen will text each of you, so be sure to check your cell phones before you come over here."

Merit badge! Of course. But when had Sean become a Boy Scout adviser? It was becoming more evident than ever that she and Sean had grown far apart during the winter months while she'd been away at school.

"How's your mom doing, Matt?"

Jumping at the chance to stay busy until Sean had a free moment to speak with her, Tessa helped the boy pick up the easel and black markers that he'd knocked onto the patio.

The boy shrugged. "She's good."

"Is she still working at the Rocklin Diner?"

Anyone who had eaten at Megan's restaurant knew Cathy Morton. Since last summer, when Megan had started catering meals to the wildfire crews, business had been booming. Megan had hired extra staff and even increased her hours of operation at the diner. She now stayed open late at night during the summer tourist season.

Matt nodded. "Yeah, she works every extra hour of overtime she can get. It's been hard since my dad died."

Hmm. No doubt Cathy needed the extra money to make ends meet. "She's a good mom. You be sure to help her out whenever you can."

"Yeah, I try. I like coming over here to Sean's house when she's not at home. I got some bad grades in school, so I'm taking a summer math class. And since Sean started tutoring me, I'm pulling a B in calculus. Mom's happy because she worried I wouldn't be able to graduate from high school next spring. I owe a lot to Sean."

The boy's gaze lifted to where Sean was drowning the embers in the fire pit with a bucket of water. A haze of smoke lifted into the air as he stirred the hot coals with a shovel to make sure they were out. Tessa heard the note of respect in Matt's voice.

"You like Sean, huh?" she asked.

"Oh, yeah. If it weren't for him, I don't know where I'd be now. After Dad died, I started hanging out with some troublemakers. Mom was pretty upset about it, but Sean took hold of me and wouldn't take no for an answer. He's my big brother now. Someday I want to be a hotshot and fight wildfires just like him."

The boy's admiration caused her to blink. She remembered that Sean had always had a tender spot in his heart for orphaned boys, probably because he'd been one of them. But he'd never shown interest like this before. She was impressed that he'd become a father-figure for this boy.

"You'd make a good firefighter. Just be sure to keep your nose clean. You don't want a criminal record to mess things up for you," she advised.

The boy chuckled, his gaze darting over to where Sean was talking with Gavin. "Sean said the same thing, and I don't want to let him down. He'd chew me out if I got into any more trouble."

Tessa could just imagine. She'd worked with Sean long enough to know he wouldn't tolerate any shenanigans.

Out of her peripheral vision, she caught a glimpse of Gavin. The boy waved goodbye before turning to leave.

"Hey, Gavin! Wait up and I'll go with you," Matt called.

Gavin paused, waiting for Matt to join him. As the two boys sauntered toward the street out front, Tessa hoped Gavin wouldn't lead Matt into any more altercations with the law.

"Be good," Sean called after them with a wave of his hand.

They waved back and disappeared around the corner.

Turning, Tessa glanced at Sean again. She liked this fatherly side to him. She just hoped he wouldn't abandon these boys the way he'd abandoned her.

"Okay, let's take a look at that report." Sean blotted the front of his damp shirt with a dish towel.

Standing inside his kitchen, he tossed the towel onto the counter and took a deep inhale to steady his nerves. Owen and the boys had left. Finally, Sean could have a moment alone with Tessa.

He wouldn't have asked her to come over here if it hadn't been important. Jared Marshall had called right as Sean was leaving work today and announced that he had some extra funds available. If Sean could get him a list of necessary items, he might be able to purchase most of it. But Jared needed the list first thing in the morning. Since Tessa was responsible for maintaining the inventory logs, and Sean had a Scout meeting tonight, he'd asked her to update the information and bring it over to him.

"Here it is." She handed him a manila folder then twined her hands together, the movement telling him that she was nervous.

He stepped into the living room and spoke without looking at her. "Have a seat."

She followed him into the brightly lit room and perched on the edge of a recliner. The blinds were still open on the wide picture window, showing a warm azure sky that gleamed with the faint dusk of evening.

He sat on the sofa. As he perused the file, she leaned forward, resting her elbows on her knees. Out of his peripheral vision, he noticed she still wore her hotshot uniform. She obviously had come here right from work.

"I think what you're doing with the Scouts is amazing. What made you decide to start working with them?" she asked.

He shrugged as memories of his own childhood washed over him. "Some of the boys like Matt and Gavin don't have a father. After the way I grew up, I thought maybe I could help them."

He didn't add that he was also trying to atone for losing her brother. He couldn't bring Zach back, but maybe he could make a difference for these boys.

"Matt told me that you've really changed his life. It's great that you've taken him under your wing," she said.

"Actually, I think it's the other way around. These boys have changed me. I love being with them."

"That's nice."

He nodded and leaned back, the folder resting on his right thigh. "I remember making some of the same stupid mistakes when I was their age and wishing someone had been there to stop me."

"I'm sure their parents appreciate what you're doing."

"I think Cathy Morton needs the most help. She's doing her best to be a good mother and keep Matt on the straight and narrow path, but it's hard to raise a teenage son on your own. She reminds me of your mom."

"Yes, she does. I hear that Cathy is dating Rich Wilcox," Tessa said.

Sean nodded. "Rich is a good man. Cathy's an overworked mom who's worried about her boy. My only regret is I can't be around for Matt as much as I'd like. He's become good friends with Gavin Smith. Gavin's a nice kid, but he's got a wild streak in him. I think he's really struggling with which side he wants to be on. And right now I think it could go either way. He's quite a handful for his grandpa."

"Do you think Gavin will lead Matt astray?" Tessa asked.

"There's no telling at this point. Hopefully Matt will make a difference for Gavin. The Scouting activities help a lot. I don't want to lose either boy. I'm determined to make sure that Matt gets his Eagle Scout award. If nothing else, he has his friends here and they're focused on service projects instead of being hoodlums. And he has me. I'll do what I can for all of those boys."

"Good. I think that's great," she said, but her voice held a tinge of doubt.

An uncomfortable silence followed. So much for small talk, but it felt good to discuss these simple things with her. It seemed so normal. Chatting about their day. Speculating on the outcome. Trying to do some good in the world. It'd be so easy for Sean to let down his guard. To forget the past and pretend that everything was okay.

He reopened the folder and scanned the lists. "You think we need more goggles?"

She nodded. "I do. The guys keep losing them. And the lenses get scratched easily."

"Maybe we need to buy a better quality lens. What about more Nomex shirts and chain saws?"

"Yes, we need shirts, mostly in sizes medium and large. And some more shovels and Pulaskis, too."

He flipped the page. "Where are the hand tools listed?"

She stood and slid next to him on the couch. Reaching in front of him, she thumbed through the pages before pointing. He caught her fragrant scent. Something fresh and citrusy. Her shoulder brushed against his and her warmth sent an electric sensation zinging down his arm.

"Right here," she said. "You can see that we've dulled numerous blades on the shovels. We've sharpened them so much that they've been ground down to nubs. And we've also broken several handles. It's time to replace a number of them."

She turned the page. "And here, you can see that we need lots more files…both for sharpening the teeth on our chain saws and regular files, too."

He chuckled. "You got that right. I don't know what Harlie does to his saws, but he goes through them faster than anyone I know. Of course, he's also one of the best sawyers I've ever seen."

"Except for Zach. He could saw through anything." She laughed.

He chuckled, too. "That's true. And your report looks

better than the ones Zach used to turn in. Remember all his crazy notes and chicken scratch when he was in charge of the inventory? None of us could read his handwriting. It was insane. I was so glad when he turned the job over to you. You keep nice, tidy records."

"Yeah, I always teased Zach that he used rotten handwriting on purpose, just so that I'd give in and do the reports for him," Tessa said.

Sean's mouth quirked up on one side. "I'm afraid you're right. There wasn't a lazy bone in Zach's body, but I wouldn't put it past him to purposefully get rid of the inventory assignment."

"Neither would I."

They both laughed, not at all bothered that Zach would do such a thing. No one liked keeping the inventory list up-to-date, except that Tessa was so good at it. She seemed much more organized than the guys.

They turned and faced each other at the same time, sitting so close that Sean could see the flecks of gold in her green eyes. Her breath whispered past his chin. Then her eyes widened and she sat back. For just a moment they'd both forgotten that Zach was gone. They'd forgotten to be sad. And for those few moments it had been wonderful. Then it all came rushing back.

She scooted away. "I'm sorry."

He took a cleansing breath. "No need."

A loud silence followed.

Turning, Sean flipped through the inventory report again. Anything to avoid the look of recriminations written across her face.

"Thanks again for bringing this by," he said. "Based on the extra funds Jared said he has, he should be able to buy most of this equipment for the crew. You did a nice job."

He hoped she'd take the hint and leave.

"Yeah, anytime," she said.

She stood and stepped toward the front door. He let her go, making a pretext of reading the report. Watching her leave, he saw her hesitate, her hand resting on the knob. Out of his peripheral vision, he saw her turn and look over her shoulder at him.

He forced himself not to acknowledge her. He didn't move a muscle for long, pounding moments, but he heard the door close. Heard her start up the engine to Zach's truck and heard her drive away. Just a handful of months and she'd be out of his life for good. He had to hold on through the summer. Then he'd be free of her, and she'd be free of him. So why did that thought leave him feeling empty inside?

Chapter Seven

The following week Tessa and the rest of the crew helped with Community Cleanup Day. Happy chatter filtered through the air as people from town scavenged the area with their families, picking up trash, chopping out dead bushes and trees, working together to make their neighborhoods look nice.

As she worked, Tessa glanced over her shoulder and saw Gavin standing next to Matt, pointing with the hand saw he held. "Hey, your mom's pretty chummy with Sean."

As usual, Gavin wore his sleeveless black T-shirt, but Matt wore his Scouting uniform. The two boys were taking a breather from pruning dead limbs off a ponderosa pine tree.

The heat of the day felt oppressive and she tugged off her Nomex jacket. As she tied the sleeves around her waist, she followed the two boys' gazes. Sean stood a short distance away, talking to Cathy Morton. In her late thirties, the pretty woman's blond hair glistened in the morning sunlight. Sean's mouth curved upward and he laughed. *Laughed!* And a blaze of jealousy pierced

Tessa's heart. Not because she thought Sean and Cathy were romantically involved, but because he used to laugh like that with her.

"They're just friends," Matt said. "Mom's dating Rich Wilcox. I think they're getting pretty serious."

Gavin snorted. "That old grease monkey? You don't want him for a stepdad. What does she see in him?"

Matt frowned. When he spoke, his words sounded a bit defensive. "Nah, he's okay. He's good to Mom and me. He's a truck driver just like my dad. Sean says he's a hard worker and a good man."

"Sean says this and Sean says that. You sure like the guy," Gavin grumbled.

"Yeah, I do." Matt rested the point of his long pruning shears against a large rock, seeming oblivious that Tessa stood no more than a stone's throw away. She kept busy with her work, showing no sign that she could overhear their conversation.

"Hey, why don't we ditch this place?" Gavin said in a conspiratorial tone.

"And go where?" Matt asked.

Gavin gave a low scoff. "Anywhere but here. I'm sick of pulling weeds. Let's get out of here."

Tessa tensed, waiting for Matt's reply.

"No, I promised Sean I'd stay for four hours. I'm working on another merit badge. I can't quit now."

"Ah, who cares what Sean thinks? We can slip away and no one will even notice that we're gone," Gavin prodded.

Matt shook his head. "Sean and Mom would notice. You do what you want, but I'm staying. I want my merit badge."

Bravo! Tessa was so relieved to hear Matt stand up for what was right.

Gavin creased his mouth in a look of disgust. "Well, I'm not working on a merit badge. I'm outta here. I'll catch you later."

Without waiting for Matt's reply, Gavin hurried up the side of the embankment to the road. Glancing around to make sure he wasn't spotted, he ducked behind the big trucks, hiding himself from view. Tessa pretended not to notice. His furtive movements attested that he wanted to make his escape without discovery. Matt stared after him, a look of half betrayal and half disappointment filling his eyes.

Tessa was about to praise him for his good choice when he turned and climbed out of the embankment toward the trucks parked alongside the road.

Was he leaving, too? Tessa held her breath, raking leaves into a tidy pile. From lowered lashes, she watched as Matt paused at the back of a truck. He retrieved a bottle of water out of the ice chest, popped the lid and downed the liquid in several long swallows. When he was done, he tossed the empty bottle into the recycle bin then gazed at a drip torch sitting on the ground nearby. Tessa had seen Ace put it there earlier. It was faulty, leaking fuel out of the nozzle even when it was turned off.

Matt picked up the torch and Tessa didn't hesitate. Earlier that morning Sean had told the boys that only the hotshots would do any of the burning. Matt had no business touching the torch. He wasn't trained on the equipment, and any misuse carried all sorts of liability issues with it. In this dry vegetation, it wouldn't take much to start a fire burning out of control.

"Matt," she called.

But too late. He lit the torch and it immediately dripped fire onto the cuff of his blue jeans. With a cry of surprise, he dropped the torch. A dribble of fire spread into the tall, dry grass along the roadside.

"Sean!" Tessa yelled to get his attention.

Matt screamed. He flailed about, his eyes wide with fear as he ran down the road, the flame on his pant cuff whipping around his ankle.

Barely conscious of Sean and Cathy hurrying toward them, Tessa whipped the Nomex jacket off from around her waist and lunged for Matt, tackling him. The hard ground slammed up to meet her. She landed on her right side, grappling with the thrashing boy. Pain shot through Tessa's rib cage, but she fought to keep her hold on Matt. She blanketed the flames with the retardant cloth, snuffing out the fire. In the process, Matt's booted foot clipped her jaw. Rockets of pain erupted from her face, and stars filled her eyes. Shaking her head, she blinked, trying to clear her dazed mind.

Strong hands lifted her up. The left side of her jaw throbbed unbearably.

"Are you okay?" Sean knelt beside her, cradling her close to his chest. His strength surrounded her. For the first time in a long time, she felt so safe.

She gazed up at him in wonder. His eyes were crinkled with concern, but another wave of pain made it difficult for her to focus.

"You sure got clobbered. Are you all right?" He lifted his hand to her face, his calloused palm gentle and warm. He was her boss. It was his job to check on her. It didn't mean anything. Not to him, and certainly not to her.

"Can you talk to me, Tess? Who am I?" he asked.

"Sean Nash. I'm fine," she said, her voice sounding tense and strange to her ears.

She pulled away so she could sit up, knowing this wasn't right. Trying to make sense out of it all. Trying to ignore the comforting safety of his arms. Her head was spinning, her heart hammering. And she honestly didn't know if it was because Sean was holding her or because she'd been kicked in the face. Once more, this man was turning her world upside down. She'd thought he couldn't hurt her anymore. That her shattered heart was too broken to feel any more pain. But she was wrong. He didn't love her anymore. And she didn't love him. So why couldn't she get her feelings under control?

"Oh, thank you, Tessa."

Cathy Morton was crouched nearby, bending over Matt. The boy sat on the ground, the tattered hem of his pant leg pushed up above his knee. His boot and sock lay beside him, his foot bare. The flesh of his ankle and calf looked completely unharmed.

"There are no burns. I can't believe it. You saved my boy," Cathy said.

"Yeah, thanks, Tessa," Matt said, his eyes shimmering with amazement and gratitude.

Tessa sat up and blinked. Sean helped her stand. She staggered, but his strong hand on her arm steadied her. She pulled free, not wanting him to touch her. Wishing she were anywhere but here.

Several people stood around gawking uselessly. Little kids hugged close to their parents' sides, their eyes round with shock. Tessa didn't care. She just wanted to get away from Sean's penetrating gaze.

"Are you okay, Matt?" she asked the boy, desperate to divert attention away from herself.

He nodded, a sheepish smile on his face. "I'm sorry I lit the torch. I thought I could do it. I just wanted to help, but I won't ever do that again."

Along the side of the road, Tessa could see several of her team members shoveling dirt over the fire that Matt had caused. They'd contained the flames, but a couple of them tossed looks of disgust in Matt's direction. She knew what they were thinking. Matt had been thoughtless. The kind of kid who frequently started wildfires out of carelessness.

"I think you've learned a valuable lesson today. Don't play around with fire," Sean said.

"I sure did. I'm sorry for all the problems I've caused." A note of sincerity filled the boy's voice.

"I'm just glad you're okay." Cathy hugged her son, smoothing a jagged thatch of hair that fell over his high forehead.

Tessa nodded and showed a half smile then leaned against the pumper truck. Chris brought the first-aid kit and cleaned the scratches on her face.

Sean eyed her with a dubious frown. "I saw Matt clip your face with his foot. Can you move your jaw?"

She opened and closed her mouth and moved it around to test its soundness. "Yes. It's sore, but not broken."

Resting his hands on his hips, Sean frowned. "You may have a nasty bruise after this. Maybe you should sit down for a little while longer, just to make sure you're okay."

She backed up a step. "No, I'm good. It's nothing a

couple of aspirin won't handle. I... I'm just glad Matt's all right."

"He'll be fine, thanks to you," Sean said. "You got to him before he suffered any injuries. It's a good thing diesel fuel burns so slow. A few more seconds and we'd have been rushing him to the hospital with some severe burns."

She nodded, pressing a trembling hand against her aching face.

"Are you really okay?" he asked.

She nodded again, but she didn't look at him. She feared he'd see the truth in her eyes. That she wasn't all right and it had nothing to do with her aching jaw.

"You did well today," Sean continued. "You always were quick on your feet. Always steady during a crisis."

Tessa didn't know how to handle his praise. It felt too intimate. Confusion filled her mind. After all, he had been the one to push her away.

He reached for the drip torch that had caused all the damage, and Tessa noticed that his hands were visibly shaking. How odd. Maybe he was more upset than he led on.

"What about you? Are you all right?" she asked.

He tensed, setting the torch inside the back of a truck where it couldn't do any more damage. Then he settled his hands on his lean hips. "Of course. Why do you ask?"

His face looked hard as chiseled granite. Hmm. Maybe she'd imagined his duress.

"No reason. I'd like to get back to work now," she said.

He turned away and she breathed a sigh of relief.

"I think you're done for the day. We're about finished

anyway. The guys will mop up and we'll go home. I want you to just sit here and rest," he said.

He didn't wait for her response but walked over to help the men. Tessa watched him go, thinking she was losing her mind. She knew the crew would make sure the fire was really out, then they'd load up their equipment and return to base. She thought about helping but decided to stay right where she was. Right now all she wanted was to lie down in a dark room and close her eyes.

How could Sean act so normal? Like nothing had happened between them. A part of her wanted to hug him, and part of her wanted to slap him. Her plan to keep her distance was proving to be more difficult than she previously thought.

Sean pushed his red helmet back on his head and wiped his brow with his forearm. The small fires they'd lit for the Community Cleanup Project had added heat to an already baking day. Another half hour and they could all go home.

He walked with Cathy and Matt to their car. Once they were both inside, he leaned against the open window on the driver's side.

"You'll make sure that she's okay, won't you?" Cathy said, looking to where Tessa sat on the running board of one of the trucks.

"Of course," Sean said.

Thankfully, Tessa hadn't lost consciousness, or he would have insisted on taking her to the hospital. But he'd been worried about her. So worried that he'd done the stupidest thing yet. He'd cradled her in his arms as waves of fear had pulsed over him. When he'd seen her fall, he'd been so scared. So afraid that she might have a concussion or a broken jaw.

"I'm so glad I got the day off work from the restaurant. It was important for me to be here. Thanks again, for everything," Cathy said.

"Yeah, thanks, Sean. And I'm truly sorry." Matt spoke quietly, his face flushed red with humiliation.

"I know, Matt. Next time be sure to think before you act," Sean said.

The boy nodded and Sean felt like a hypocrite. He should have thought about his actions before he had embraced Tessa. But he'd been so worried about her. And when the fire had spread, a thick panic had clogged his throat. His men had quickly encircled the blaze and controlled it, but not before thoughts of the day Zach had died came rushing back to Sean, making him tremble.

He and Zach had been surrounded by fire, shut off from escape. He'd begged Zach to follow him, but the man had screamed in fear, just like Matt had done. And then Zach had run the wrong way. He'd panicked, his eyes filled with scalding terror. And this was the first fire Sean had experienced since that horrible day.

"Sean, are you all right?" Cathy asked.

His expression must have given him away. He forced himself to smile and push aside his morose thoughts. "Sure. I'm fine. I'm just glad no one got seriously injured today."

"Me, too."

He nodded and stood back as she started the engine and drove away. His hands were shaking and he slid them into his pants pockets so no one would notice. It was times like this when his PTSD reared its ugly head. But he could control it. He knew he could. He must!

Maybe his promise to keep Tessa safe had been futile. Even on a simple cleanup exercise like this, she could have been badly injured. Maybe he wasn't the right man for this superintendent job. Maybe he shouldn't fight wildfires anymore. But he had to, for Tessa's sake. If he could just make it to the end of this fire season, she'd be gone and he could move on. It was time. Wasn't it?

Sean glanced over at his crewmen and caught Tessa watching him. The moment their eyes met, she jerked and looked away. Her face flushed a pretty shade of pink and he knew she was embarrassed to be caught staring at him.

He wondered what she was thinking. What she was feeling. And more than anything, he wished he could ease her pain. He wished he could explain everything to her, but she wouldn't understand. And Sean could never explain to Tessa that he'd abandoned Zach and chosen life instead.

Chapter Eight

Tessa closed her eyes, trying to sleep. Even burdened by her heavy Nomex shirt and high-topped fire boots, she could sleep anywhere most of the time. But not this night. Not aboard this cumbersome school bus.

They'd finished the community service project, returned to their hotshot base and got cleaned up just in time to get called out on a wildfire in California.

Lifting a hand, she wiped her damp brow. All the windows on the bus were lowered, but the evening breeze did little to relieve the oppressive heat. The sound of the engine deepened as the vehicle crawled up the narrow road circling Nesbitt Pass in the Sierra Nevada Mountains. At over eight thousand feet elevation, this would be their first real wildfire of the season. Tessa's stomach swooped and dipped over every twisting bend in the road. At this stealthy pace, it'd be another hour before they reached the fire camp high in the mountain forest above Splendor Lake. But that wasn't what bothered her.

Huddled in her seat, she cracked open an eye and peered through the shadows at the front of the bus.

Sean sat near the driver, his head up and eyes open, one strong hand resting casually along the top of the seat in front of him as he gazed out the dark windshield. Stars glittered in the moonless sky, the shadows clinging to his chiseled profile. His tall body swayed with the erratic thumps of the bus. Now and then he spoke to the driver, his deep voice lost within the low drone of the engine. Every other member of her crew lay slumped across the cracked padded seats, their gear and tools stowed beside them for a quick grab once the vehicle stopped. Apparently Sean didn't need sleep as much as the rest of the team.

She couldn't stop thinking of the fervent way he'd embraced her when Matt had accidentally kicked her in the face. He'd said he didn't want her anymore, but his actions spoke differently. So what was going on? If he didn't want her, what did he want? He hadn't made any changes to his life that she could see. Maybe he didn't even know what he wanted. She told herself she didn't care, but it firmed her resolve to stay as far away from him as possible.

Shaking her head, she closed her eyes again. The driver shifted down. The vehicle slowed and Tessa opened her eyes. Looking out the window, she caught sight of the generator lights at base camp. An open alpine meadow filled with tents, water tankers, pumper trucks and other fire equipment. Even at this late hour, a melee of firefighters moved across the clearing in a beehive of organized chaos.

The bus came to a jarring stop.

"Everyone out," Sean called.

The crew members groaned and sat up, rubbing their sleepy eyes. Tessa knew the drill. Latching on to her pack, she scanned the floor beneath her seat to ensure she didn't leave something behind. The rest of the crew did likewise, perched on the edge of their seats as they waited for the driver to open the door and let them out.

One by one, the men stood and walked the thin aisle. Tessa followed, staring straight ahead. Conscious of Sean's gaze following her as she passed by, she forced herself not to lift a hand up to her face. Matt's boot had left an ugly bruise there, but it would soon fade. If only her heartache would disappear as quickly.

Sean was the last man off the bus, ensuring his crew was awake and assembled.

"Relax. I'll be right back," he said.

He placed his red helmet on his head, flattening his dark, curly hair. He sauntered toward a cluster of men wearing white and red hard hats to signify their administrative status. They milled around a table set up beneath an open-air tent.

Tessa watched as the supervisory team studied a map beneath the glow of lamplight. They gestured and nodded at each other. Sean leaned against the table, looking casual. Tessa wasn't fooled. He was highly alert and ready to move. Nodding one last time, he walked back to the crew.

"Okay, listen up. We've got a lightning-caused fire of about five thousand acres. Three other hotshot crews are already working on the mountain, but more will come in later this morning from Idaho and Montana. The fire is twenty percent contained." He jutted his chin toward a sturdy table set up with Cubitainer jugs of water and brown sack lunches that had been prepared for them by a caterer.

"If you need it, you've got three minutes to water

up and collect your lunch. Then we're going on a little stroll," Sean said.

Several members of the crew groaned. A stroll meant they had a long, arduous hike ahead of them. Staggering to their feet, the team ambled over to top off their canteens. Tessa joined them. As she snatched up a sack lunch to stow away in her pack, no one said a word.

Lifting her chin, she met Sean's gaze. He hovered near the crew like a mother hen. He was in charge and the safety of this entire team rested on his overly broad shoulders. She just hoped they could trust him to make good judgments that got them all home safely.

"Let's rock and roll," Sean called.

With his pack on his back, he headed toward the trees. The crew affixed their lamps to the fronts of their hard hats and hustled after him. Tessa fell in line at the back of the pack.

Moving through the trees with only their flashlights to guide them, they soon found themselves hiking up a steep, narrow trail lined with oaks and pines. In the starlight, Tessa could make out the eerie movement of white, drifting smoke that had settled across the mountain. She climbed steadily, her thigh muscles burning with her exertions.

"You doing okay?"

Snapping around, she ran headfirst into Sean's wide chest. He reached out to steady her, his strong hands closing over her arms. Currents of electricity pulsed between them. For several stunned moments her eyes locked with his.

Feeling burned by his touch, she jerked away and kept going. "I'm fine."

She didn't need him to pamper her. After all, she was a veteran wildfire fighter. A hotshot!

The pungent odor of sweat and smoke filled the air. She could hear Sean moving down the line, checking on the other men. She imagined his shrewd gaze assessing each of them, to determine their well-being. And then a nibble of guilt chewed at her conscience. He hadn't singled her out when he'd asked if she was okay. He was just doing his job, watching out for his crew. Maybe she was being overly sensitive.

"Okay, huddle up," Sean called.

The team gathered close.

"Those granite rocks above look like a good place for a safety zone. A sudden wind shift and we could find ourselves eating fire. Anyone not know our escape route?" He pointed to the hillside above and they all turned to study the area.

Hmm. Tessa couldn't help being impressed. At least Sean was putting their safety first. Maybe he had learned a hard lesson from his experience with Zach. Maybe it had made him more cautious. But the price had been way too high.

Sean gestured to his two squad leaders. Each one had nine men serving under him. The three bosses checked their radios to ensure they had good communication.

"We're gonna anchor right here and cut line fifteen feet wide and head toward that outcropping of granite." Sean pointed at a projection of gray rock a mile away. "The Black Mountain hotshots are gonna come in behind us and widen our line out another ten feet."

Tessa didn't need to ask why. Once the fire awakened with the heat from the afternoon sunlight, it would start moving up this mountain. For them to have to cut a line fifteen feet wide and then have another hotshot crew cut an additional ten feet, it meant the flames of the fire must be burning at fifteen feet high. The line had to be wide enough that the blaze couldn't jump over it.

"All right, let's fight fire." Sean clapped his gloved hands twice.

The crew lined out, waiting for the sawyers and swampers to open the canopy of trees so the rest of the crew could follow behind. Tessa tugged on her leather gloves then joined their two toolers, helping them toss debris far away from the fireline. The persistent buzz of chain saws filled the air along with the clops of chopping out roots and hacking at the thick litter of duff covering the ground.

Every time she turned, Tessa found Sean working nearby, like a sentinel determined to protect her. Surely she imagined his constant attention. He wasn't staying close by her on purpose. Or was he?

His beautiful blue eyes lifted and rested on her like a leaden weight. So intense that she felt his gaze piercing her to the back of her spine.

Tessa whirled away, trying her best to ignore him.

She was watching him. Sean could feel Tessa's eyes boring a hole in the back of his head.

He turned and caught the flash of anger in her gaze. Eyes that had once crinkled with laughter and love now showed her irritation. For him. He hated the accusation he saw on her face. The doubt and pain. He'd broken her heart and she might never forgive him.

She bent her back over her Pulaski as she scraped the earth down to mineral soil, able to work most men under the table. As usual, she'd pulled her long, golden-brown hair back in a ponytail. A few shimmering wisps escaped the confines of her yellow hard hat and framed her delicate profile. No matter how much sun she got, her skin gleamed like alabaster, not a freckle in sight.

He longed to call out to her. To tease and joke with her the way they used to do when they were working. But after what had happened at the community cleanup the day before, he didn't dare get any closer than necessary. He'd vowed to keep her safe, but the dark bruise on her face attested that he'd failed. His feelings were on the surface and he feared he might reveal his inner doubts. Instead, he walked farther down the line, focusing on the entire crew, clenching his hands so no one would notice that they were trembling. His pulse sped up as his gaze scanned every member of the squad. He made mental calculations to ensure they all were accounted for and in good shape. But what if he couldn't keep them that way? What if something bad happened? Something out of his control.

By ten in the morning, he called for the team to halt and eat lunch. They sat below the steep ridge above and opened their brown sacks. No one spoke as they wolfed down smashed ham sandwiches, red apples, strips of beef jerky, bags of roasted almonds and boxes of juice.

Sean exhaled a long breath of relief. They'd made it this far without any mishaps. But the day was far from over with. Conscious of their surroundings, he noticed the fire had crawled up the mountain, trailing them, but not too close. Above all else, he wanted enough time to evacuate his crew to the safety zone, if necessary.

"Tank, you'll plant it over on that ridge and serve as our lookout. You should be able to see what the fire is doing from that vantage point and give us plenty of warning if we're in danger." Sean pointed toward the north.

A veteran firefighter, Tank was big and bull-strong. Sean hated to lose the man's strength on the fireline right now but knew he could rely on him not to fall asleep on the job. That would leave the team exposed to danger.

Popping the last bit of a granola bar into his mouth, Tank crunched down and nodded before gathering up his gear so he could move into position. Before he left the group, Sean had him test his radio. No taking risks. He'd learned firsthand that putting out a forest fire was never worth a man's life.

The team returned to work, hacking at the ground in numbing monotony. Sean glanced Tessa's way. She popped the lid off a tube of lip balm, slathered it on her lips then slid the tube back into her pants pocket.

Sean smiled, remembering the taste of her raspberry lip gloss the night before Zach had died. The three of them had eaten dinner together. Then Sean had taken Tessa for a walk alone. Beneath the canopy of moonlight, he'd pulled her into his arms and she'd whispered that she loved him. He'd kissed her. One of the best memories of his life.

A crashing sound came from behind. Whirling around, Sean stared in horror as a flaming eighty-foot ponderosa pine fell toward Tessa and Pete, one of their sawyers.

"Look out!" A flare of adrenaline pushed Sean into action. Dropping his Pulaski, he sprinted toward Tessa as the blazing tree smashed into another pine. The two trees swayed together, flames sparking and dancing in the air. As if in slow motion, the trees picked up momentum, hurtling toward the earth.

"Move!" Sean bellowed as he ran, frantically waving his arms at the crew members in his path.

Everyone scrambled madly to get out of the way. They had only seconds to react. The thunderous crash of the trees shook the ground.

Sean leaped down into the burning brush, clawing his way toward Tessa. Desperate to reach her. A cloud of dust enveloped him, so thick and heavy that he choked and blinked his eyes. He couldn't see. He didn't know where to turn. Where was she?

A man's piercing scream of pain caused Sean to spin about. The air cleared just a bit and he saw Pete lying beneath the melee of heavy tree limbs. The tree had barely missed Tessa, who was trying to pull Pete out. Flames ignited all around, rushing toward them. So hot and furious that Sean felt the scorching heat against his face. And his mind flooded with relief. Tessa was okay. She was safe. For now.

"Over here," Sean yelled to the rest of the crew.

Hacking at the tree limbs with his ax, he broke Pete free. The fire lapped at the fallen man's feet. Tessa shoveled dirt over the flames. Gripping Pete's shoulders, Sean pulled him free. Extra hands reached to assist Sean. The crew was finally here.

Pete moaned and thrashed his head from side to side. "Get me out of here," he cried.

Half of the squad surrounded and attacked the fire, snuffing it out. Sean was conscious of Tessa helping, working frantically with the rest of the team.

Several men helped Sean lift Pete and carry him out of harm's way. After they'd laid him on the ground,

Sean knelt over him, checking his vital signs. The yellow sleeve of Pete's Nomex shirt was damp with blood.

"Get the first-aid kit," Sean ordered, a blaze of urgency sizzling up his spine.

The kit appeared before him. Tessa had already retrieved it. No need to ask her twice.

Pete coughed, his breath raspy.

In a rush, the memory of the fire that had killed Zach bludgeoned Sean's mind. So swift and powerful that it made him gasp. Then he clenched his hands, reminding himself to think. To breathe. To keep moving.

"You okay, buddy?" Sean forced himself to speak calmly as he reached for his pocket knife. Although it didn't show, his hands were quaking and he was fighting a rush of panic that seemed to clog his chest. Of all the times for his PTSD to act up, now wasn't it. He had to maintain control. Had to appear confident and make good decisions. His entire crew was counting on him.

"My side hurts." Pete spoke in a hoarse croak.

Possibly some broken ribs. Sean flipped out the knife blade and slit the sleeve of Pete's shirt up to the shoulder. The man had an ugly compound fracture. Not good.

Sean glanced at Tessa. She watched him with narrowed eyes and he felt self-conscious. He was worried that she might detect how the PTSD still affected him. And he didn't want her to know. Didn't want anyone to think he wasn't fit for command. Because he was. He must be.

He stared at the injured man, momentarily frozen in place. His thoughts scattered and he couldn't make sense of it all. What was wrong with him? Why had he promised Zach that he'd keep Tessa safe? What had made him ever think he could protect her?

"Sean, are you all right?"

She knelt beside him, performing triage on Pete. She paused for a moment, peering at Sean with concern. Seeing the unease in her eyes brought him back to sanity. She was counting on him. They all were. For some strange reason, knowing she was here and depending on him gave him the courage to keep going. He mustn't let her down. He mustn't fail again.

"Yes, I'm… I'm okay," he said.

"You know it's gonna be okay. Right?" she asked.

He took comfort from her words. "Yeah. Of course it is."

Yes. Focus on the job. That was what he needed to do.

A roll of bandages appeared in front of his nose. Trained as a medic, Tessa knew what to do. Sean snatched up the bandages and nodded his gratitude. And then he concentrated on the situation. But he couldn't help feeling surprised that she was comforting him. He thought he was her guardian, not the other way around. She had no reason to be kind to him, and yet she was.

Together, they staunched the blood and kept Pete's wound as clean as possible. Tessa treated Pete for shock then dressed a mild laceration on his forehead. The tourniquet on his arm should hold until they could evacuate him. Knowing each of his crew member's strengths, Sean rattled off orders as he worked. He called to his squad leaders, assured that they'd coordinate their men to get the job done.

"Harlie, you radio command. Tell them to get us a chopper to evacuate Pete. And don't take no for an answer. Tell them it's critical. Chris, we need a stretcher.

Get your squad to make one now. Tess, you check Pete's ribs for a punctured lung."

The team didn't have to be told twice. They went to work. No one sat idle. Everyone hustled. And Sean had never loved his crew members more than in that moment.

He exhaled slowly. He was holding it together. He could do this. He must do this!

"Pete definitely has a punctured lung," Tessa said.

Not good, but it was better than a collapsed lung.

Her fingers brushed against Sean's. She snapped her hand back, her gaze meeting his. They stared at one another for just a moment, but that look spoke volumes. Confusion and uncertainty filled her expressive eyes.

Harlie stood back and clutched his black radio. "I've got the command base. Where do you want them to land the chopper?"

Sean glanced at the heavy vegetation surrounding them. No safe location nearby, so they'd just have to make a place.

He jutted his chin and pointed up. "That ridge over our heads. We'll go up there. It'll be the quickest way to get Pete off of this mountain."

All eyes turned upward, toward the rocky plateau. It rose almost straight up over them, the hillside covered with thick vegetation they'd have to hack their way through. And in a fraction of a moment, Sean knew what he was asking his team to do. It was a gargantuan task under the best of circumstances. And as tired as they all were, they now had to act fast. No time to waste. No time to be tired.

"Okay, you heard the super. Let's clear a path to that ridge." Chris pointed the way.

Retrieving their chain saws, the sawyers attacked the thick brush. Two other men helped clear the debris out of the path. The roar of saws filled the air along with the acrid scent of wood smoke.

"He's got at least two broken ribs," Tessa reported.

Pete groaned, his eyes clenched tightly shut. "It hurts."

"I know, buddy. But we're gonna fix you up fine. We'll get you out of here. You're gonna be okay. You have my word," Sean promised.

Pete gave a slight nod, taking another scratchy breath.

Sean helped Tessa wrap the injured man's midsection to stabilize his rib cage. Over the noise of the saws, static squawked on the radio.

"Hey! I saw the trees fall. Are you guys okay down there?" Tank asked from his lookout point.

No! Sean wanted to yell. Pete wasn't okay. But he would be. And so would Tessa and the rest of the crew. Sean would make sure of that. If he had to give his life in the process, he would accept nothing less.

Chapter Nine

What was wrong with Sean? Tessa's gaze swept over him. He knelt over Pete, his hands shaking like aspen leaves in the wind. The power of his expression caused Tessa to freeze. His pledge to keep Pete safe softened something inside her, and a lance of emotion pierced her heart. He seemed a bit shaken, and yet he was acting perfectly rational, making all the right decisions, putting the safety of the crew first. But something was wrong.

She'd never seen Sean like this. Focused and composed, yet so potent that it almost frightened her. Too calm and unruffled. Too intense. As though he was terrified, yet forcing himself to keep going.

When the trees had fallen, everyone had run for cover. Everyone except Sean.

She'd been so scared. Watching those giant burning trees hurtling toward her, she'd scurried out of the way as fast as her legs could move. While she'd cried out a silent prayer for help, Sean had yelled and plunged into the fray. Hurrying to reach her and Pete. Strong and invincible.

Putting his own life on the line to save them.

For the first time, a thought occurred to Tessa. Had Sean fought this hard to save Zach? Or was he taking unnecessary risks again? Sean had always been a daredevil. An adrenaline junkie who thrived on the edge of danger. Never had he backed away from fire. His courage made him a great firefighter. But now she didn't know what to think. His actions were those of a good, safe leader. Had she misjudged him? Was he innocent of any poor judgment that had gotten Zach killed?

A burst of static came from the radio. Tank was waiting for news.

Harlie pressed the call button and reported. "Pete's hurt. We're evacuating him along the ridge."

"Ask him what the fire is doing." Sean barked the order.

Harlie lifted the radio to his mouth and relayed Sean's question to Tank. A brief pause of static followed.

"No danger," Tank reported. "The fire's broiling down below but hasn't moved much. You've got time. I've got your back."

Bless Tank. Tessa knew he'd watch out for them so that they could focus on Pete. Unless a squirrely wind pushed the fire in their direction, they had time. Thanks to Sean's quick thinking.

Chris's squad retrieved two strong tree limbs and sliced the small branches off them. Then the men removed their sturdy Nomex shirts. Wearing their blue T-shirts, they slid the sleeves of their Nomex over the tree limbs to create a makeshift stretcher.

"The chopper is on its way!" Harlie yelled.

Within minutes they had Pete loaded on the stretcher and ready to go. But clearing a path to the ridge above wasn't so easy.

"Stay with him, Tess," Sean advised.

His gaze locked with hers and he paused for just a fraction of time. In his eyes she saw a brief spark of apprehension. Then he flashed that reckless smile of his. So masculine, so handsome. A flicker of emotion filled his eyes, so fierce that she had to blink. He lifted a hand toward her. For two whole seconds she thought he might pull her in close and kiss her. And for those two seconds she wished that he would. To pretend that nothing bad had happened between them. To forget the past and feel his solid arms around her once more. Then he turned and was gone, and she thought she must have imagined it all.

She shook her head. What was she thinking? She didn't care about this man anymore. She didn't love him. He was her boss, nothing more. Right?

Behind her, she heard Sean calling more orders as the men cleared the trail. She centered her attention on Pete, keeping him calm. Easing him any way that she could. Speaking to him in a soothing voice. Giving him hope.

She glanced up and watched as Sean assaulted the hillside with the rest of the crew. And once they had a thin path cleared, Sean's six strongest men picked up the stretcher and carried Pete's weight on their shoulders. Holding tight, they walked straight up with the rest of the team literally pushing them from behind. Tessa joined her team, thrusting against the man in front of her with all her might. Fighting to keep her footing in the loose soil and rocks.

The sound of a chopper permeated her consciousness. From her peripheral vision, she caught the whirl of the craft's blades overhead.

Almost there.

Gritting her teeth, she shoved hard. By the time they reached the evacuation site, they all gasped and staggered to catch their breath. Tessa's arms shook with fatigue. Her legs felt like wet noodles.

The chopper touched down on the rocky plateau, spewing wind and dirt in her eyes. The door slid open and two men hopped out and ran to help load Pete.

"Tess, you go to the hospital with Pete. Stay with him," Sean ordered, breathing hard.

She swung around and stared at him, her mouth dropping open, her eyes wide with surprise.

"But I'm not his partner. Dean should go with him," she said.

Why would Sean send her away like this? It wasn't the norm. And she couldn't help feeling like he was banishing her from the mountain.

The crew stood watching her, their shoulders slumped as the adrenaline pumping in their bodies slowed now that they'd met their goal. In their bloodshot eyes, Tessa caught their censure. Most of them knew her history with Sean, but that didn't matter. Not here, not now. Safety came first and this wasn't the time to argue with the superintendent. Not when Pete's life hung in the balance. Not when they had fought so hard to save him.

"You're lighter than the other men and won't bog the chopper down with unnecessary weight. I want you to go with him," Sean said.

Tessa met Sean's eyes, searching for the truth. His reasoning seemed sound, except that this large aircraft could hold many more men. So why? Why was Sean sending her away?

For a fleeting moment a memory of her father pushing her away filled her mind. She'd been seven years old when she'd hugged his waist and begged him not to leave her. Without a word, he'd thrust her aside, turned around and walked out of her life without looking back. Tessa knew, because she'd watched to see if he would.

And then Sean had done the same thing. Breaking off their engagement when Zach had died. Abandoning her to the grief consuming her heart.

He didn't want her.

Sean looked away, ignoring her. He didn't love her anymore. No, he wanted her gone. Out of his sight. But the crew might misconstrue his actions as preferential treatment. And she didn't want that. Not from anyone. She'd worked too hard to make herself a part of this team. But she shut her mouth and did as ordered. Turning, she ran to the chopper. Climbing on board, she scooted into her seat and buckled up.

As the door slid closed, she flinched. Feeling shut off from her team. Feeling like an outcast. Like she didn't belong.

She stared out the window at her crewmates. Men she'd laughed with and worked beside for the past four years.

The aircraft lifted off, but she continued to gaze down below as the men got smaller, like plastic toy dolls. She saw Sean calling them together, clapping his hand on their backs. In her mind, Tessa could hear his deep voice as he praised their good work. Telling them he was proud of them. That they'd done a great job.

They all needed rest, but she doubted they would get more than a few minutes. The command center was counting on them to tie in the line and they had a little less than a quarter of a mile left to go. And she longed to be down there with them. To share in this victory. But she knew someone had to go with Pete. And that someone was her.

Sitting back, she released a pent-up sigh. As the chopper zipped through the air like an elegant bird, her throat tightened. She tried to relax and failed. The notion that Sean had sent her away on purpose soaked into her mind. At the beginning of the fire season, she had thought she could handle working with him. But being close to him every day and interacting like this was taking its toll on her heart. She'd tried to be patient and take Megan's advice. To have faith. To follow her heart and give herself time to work through her grief. No doubt Sean needed to do the same. But now she didn't think this was going to work. She didn't want to be near him anymore. It was time she found another job far away from Sean and his brooding eyes.

The hollow thud of Sean's boot heels pounded against the tiled floor as he walked the long hallways of the hospital. His yellow Nomex shirt stood out like a neon sign. He ignored the stares of people as he hurried through the emergency room. He felt self-conscious, stinking of smoke, his face and firefighting clothes black with soot. He must look a sight, but he couldn't wait another moment. It had been six hours since he'd seen Tessa. The last report he'd received on the mountain by radio had said that Pete would soon be out of surgery. Sean had to check on his man. He also had to see Tessa and know that she was all right.

At the nurses' station, he glanced around at the sterile equipment. "Excuse me, please."

"May I help you?" A staff member stood holding

a manila folder in her hands. Her gaze flickered over Sean's grungy attire with repugnance.

"They brought my man in here," he said.

"You mean the firefighter?" Another older nurse, with cottony white hair and wearing a blue smock, flashed a helpful smile.

"Yes," he said.

"Come with me." She walked around the front counter.

He followed as she turned the corner and led him down another hallway, past a small waiting area. The air smelled of antiseptic and overcooked beef stew. A persistent beep sounded from inside one of the rooms.

"Here we are." The nurse stopped in front of the men's restroom.

At Sean's curious glance, she reached for two coarse towels sitting on a cart against the wall.

"Wash up first, then you can go in there and visit your friend." She pointed at a room walled by window partitions and white curtains pulled closed so he couldn't see inside.

Okay, he'd been told. Nodding, he stepped inside the restroom, closed the door and scrubbed his face and hands. Rivulets of black ran down the white porcelain sink. He tried to rinse it away, but the tar refused to budge. Without cleanser, he couldn't clean it off. Some custodian was going to hate him for this.

Drying himself off, Sean glanced in the mirror at the heavy stubble on his face. Tessa hadn't liked him in a beard because it poked her whenever he had cuddled her. Even though they weren't together anymore, he planned to shave his face the first chance he got. He grimaced at the soot still clinging to his curly hair. No wonder he was still single at the age of thirty-one. Not many women would put up with his lifestyle and dangerous profession. Not unless she was another hotshot who understood the demands.

A woman like Tessa.

That would all change after this summer, when he took an office management job. Instead of taking off to fight a wildfire for weeks at a time, he'd be home most evenings. He'd have time to mow the lawn and watch TV. He'd lead a sedentary, boring life. But maybe some other woman would want him then. The problem was, they wouldn't be Tessa.

When he walked back into the hallway, he came face-to-face with her. Her mouth rounded in surprise and they stared at one another for several pounding moments. His gaze feasted on the sight of her. She also wore her Nomex shirt, but she'd washed and combed her hair. Even without makeup, she looked beautiful. And knowing she was safe brought instant respite to his worried mind.

"Hi, there," he said.

She shrugged. "The nurse told me you were here."

"Yeah, I came to check on Pete."

And you. But he didn't say that out loud.

"How is he doing?" Sean asked.

"He's out of surgery and stable. He's gonna be okay. You can go in, but he's sleeping. His parents and fiancée will be here anytime now."

Relief washed over Sean and he bumped against the wall. He jerked away so his filth wouldn't rub off on the pristine paint.

"How about you? Are you doing all right?" he asked.

"Yeah, I'm just dandy," she said.

Her clipped response told him she didn't want to talk. But that didn't diminish his concern for her.

"Have you eaten? Have you slept?" he asked.

She clenched her teeth. "Stop with the questions already. I'm fine."

"Tess, I'm not asking you any questions I wouldn't ask my other crew members," he said.

Her gaze slid to the floor. "I know. It's just been a long two days. Do you want me back on the line now?"

"No, the fire has been contained."

"Good."

"I'm sorry about sending you away. I know it bothered you, but I thought it was for the best."

"Save it!" She slashed the air with her hand, and a flare of rebellion filled her stunning green eyes. "You don't owe me any explanations...for that. You're the boss. You did what you had to do. Let's just drop it."

As the superintendent of their crew, he knew he didn't need to explain his decisions to her. And yet he felt as though he must. But right now, facing her scowl, he couldn't speak the words sweltering in his heart. She was still hurting over his rejection.

Placing his hands in his pants pockets, he sidled past her toward the door, feeling like a naughty little kid. Not a fully grown man in charge of an entire crew of hotshots. "Guess I better go in now. When I'm done, I can give you a ride back to the command post."

"Actually, I'm leaving now. They sent someone from the fire camp to pick me up," she said.

He nodded, thinking it was best to put some distance between them. "Good. I'll see you back at base. The rest of the team is helping with the mop up. They've got your gear. We'll be leaving for home later this afternoon."

"Great." She took a step, seeming eager to escape.

He opened his mouth, but decided to let her go before he made an absolute fool of himself by saying something they both might regret.

"Bye." She gave a little wave of her hand, turned on her heels and walked fast down the hall.

Sean stared after her, wishing more than anything that he could turn back the hands of time.

Chapter Ten

Tessa sat in the forest supervisor's headquarters and gazed at the fire management officer. She felt like she faced a firing squad. The team had returned home from the wildfire yesterday, but maybe she should have waited a little longer before scheduling an appointment with the FMO. She'd told Harlie, her crew boss, that she needed some personal time to run a quick errand. He'd willingly agreed, but she'd seen the questioning look in his eyes as she'd left the hotshot base.

"What is so urgent that you wanted to see me about?" Jared Marshall sat behind his wide, faux-mahogany desk and folded his hands over his chest.

Even though Jared had married Megan a number of months ago, Tessa had no illusions. Not in the workplace. She didn't want to be here, but she felt compelled. At the beginning of the fire season, she had thought she could keep her distance and work with Sean without involving her heart. But she'd been wrong. Her conflicting emotions were driving her crazy. It was time she did something about it. She had to get away from Sean, for good this time. But it wouldn't be easy. Most hotshot crews had filled their vacancies long before she'd returned to Minoa. And being a woman starting over on a new squad of macho men meant she'd have to prove her value all over again. For that reason she'd tried to stick it out here, but now she believed a transfer would be better than this angst she was feeling around Sean.

Taking a deep breath, she spoke without stammering. "I'd like to request a transfer to another hotshot crew."

Jared's eyebrows lowered, but he didn't blink. He just stared at her with a dark, brooding gaze that told her he didn't approve.

"Why?" he finally asked.

Here it was. The big question.

"You already know my history with Sean. Do I really need to explain?" she asked.

In fact, Jared had been a good friend to both of them. But right now Jared was wearing his FMO hat and she knew he'd be nothing but professional in dealing with this situation.

He heaved a deep exhale. "Look, Tessa, it broke all of our hearts when Zach died. But firefighters understand the risks. It comes with the job. It wasn't Sean's fault. It just happened. In fact, Megan and I were caught in the same burnover with our kids. We were very blessed to make it out alive."

Tessa tightened her hands, determined to remain calm and rational. She liked that Jared referred to Megan's two young children as if they were his own. And she was so grateful they'd made it out of the fire with nothing more than a bit of smoke inhalation. If only Zach had been able to do the same.

"I understand that more than anyone," she said. "But Sean doesn't seem to get it. He broke off our engagement, yet he's so protective of me. With all that's standing between us, it's become difficult to work with him."

There, she'd said the words out loud. She'd hoped Sean might change over time. That he'd finally discuss the issue with her, but he'd refused. If he was indifferent toward her, that would be something she could handle. Something she could accept. But telling her that he didn't want her anymore, and then showering his attention on her, was driving her nuts.

Jared sat back in his leather chair, the springs squeaking in protest. "I'm sorry to hear that. Fighting fire is a hazardous profession, no matter how you look at it. And when something bad happens, we want to blame someone. But sometimes it isn't anyone's fault. The fire blows up and we hand our lives over to God."

She stared at Jared. "If Sean did nothing wrong, do you think he still blames himself anyway?"

"It's possible. I know I did. Five years ago I was a superintendent when I lost two members on my crew. I wasn't with them when it happened, but I can't help thinking I should have saved their lives somehow. It still tears me up inside. If only I could have done something to bring them home safe. I wouldn't be surprised if Sean feels the same way about Zach."

So she was right. Sean felt guilty. But what for? If he had done nothing wrong, why would he push her away? It didn't make sense to her. But she wasn't a doctor. She didn't understand the workings of a person's mind. What was simple for her to accept might be difficult for someone else.

"I'd like to take a look at Sean's personal therapy notes on Zach's death," she said.

Jared's mouth tightened. "You'd have to talk to him

about that. I've already provided you with the final incident report."

"That's not what I want to read."

"Sean's personal notes aren't for public view. They're just a bunch of scribbles anyway. Without him to translate, I doubt you'd be able to make much sense out of them."

"I'm not the public, Jared. I'm a member of this crew."

"Yes, and you're also Zach's sister. You're not thinking objectively."

"But it might help give me insight into Sean's mindset. To make sure he's not hiding something." The moment she said the words, she wished she hadn't.

Jared's eyes narrowed on her like two heat-seeking missiles. "You know that's not right. He wouldn't have been able to hide anything from the investigation team. They were too thorough. I think you're too close to the situation, Tessa. Your judgment is a bit clouded."

Really? She thought her judgment was working fine. She knew the *Watch Out* situations and the rules to fire suppression. And one of them was to avoid working in a chimney area that could funnel the fire right up to the crew. Even so, hotshots still worked in chimney areas. Even she had done it on numerous occasions, although it could be dangerous. Since everyone already knew this, she didn't understand why Sean wouldn't let her view his personal notes. The logical answer was that he was hiding something. Something big. But what could it be?

"You've known Sean a long time. Have you ever seen him do something wrong on a fire?" Jared asked.

She paused, thinking this over. Then she spoke truthfully. "No. That's why I'm trying to understand what went wrong."

"The fire went wrong, Tessa. That's all. I understand you just returned from the Splendor Fire and one of your crewmen got hurt. Was it anyone's fault?"

"No, it just happened," she said.

"That's right. Did you see Sean make any poor decisions or do something wrong on the mountain?"

She paused, remembering how he'd momentarily hesitated, a brief flash of panic in his eyes. And then the way his hands had trembled as he'd helped her wrap the bandages around Pete's wounds. But he'd been perfectly rational and in complete control of his team. His leadership had been inspiring.

"No." She chewed her bottom lip, still stinging over how he had sent her away.

"Did Sean fail to act appropriately when Pete got hurt?" Jared asked.

"No. In fact, he saved Pete's life." And if she'd been injured, she had no doubt he would have saved her, too.

"But what if Pete had died? Would it have been Sean's fault?" Jared asked.

"No, of course not."

Unless he'd failed to do everything he could to save Pete. In fact, Sean was a hero. He'd acted so fast, the rest of the crew didn't even know what was happening. Honestly, she was impressed by Sean. She always had been. She still thought he was the most handsome, dynamic man she'd ever met. And being around him was a constant reminder that she'd loved him once. That she wasn't as emotionally removed from him as she thought. And for that reason, she wanted to get away from him. Before he could break her heart again.

"So, what's the problem?" Jared lifted his eyebrows, his eyes filled with a bit of annoyance.

Tessa couldn't explain all of her feelings to Jared. On the surface, there was no problem. But saving Pete's life didn't resolve the chaos of doubts blistering her mind. The tension between her and Sean was still there.

"It's just a difficult situation," she said, feeling like a big baby who was whining too much.

He paused as though choosing his words carefully. "I understand that, Tessa. And I'm sorry, but I can't make changes to the crew every time two people don't get along."

Yes, the hotshot crew must go on. It must continue to work effectively, with or without Tessa on the team. She understood that all too well.

Jared hardened his jaw, his eyes narrowed. "If you can't get along with Sean, I'm afraid you'll have to find another job. I won't do anything to compromise this team, including shuffle firefighters around because they don't like each other. Zach's death was a terrible tragedy, but Sean was cleared of any wrongdoing. In fact, Zach was as much at fault as Sean was."

Horror ignited inside her and she peered at him, wondering what he meant. "You said it wasn't anyone's fault. Zach was just following orders. Wasn't he?"

His lips tightened as if he was trying not to say something. Was he keeping something from her, too?

He paused for a moment as though choosing his words carefully. "In the middle of a crisis, we never know how we might react. People can panic, Tessa. They can do irrational things they wouldn't normally do."

Hmm. What was he insinuating? "My brother was a seasoned firefighter. Did he do something irrational?"

He heaved a sigh of futility and shook his head. "Nothing will bring him back, Tessa."

Yes, but that didn't resolve her problem of how to continue working with Sean without feeling like her heart was breaking all over again. But Jared wasn't about to budge. Tessa could see the resolve etched in his stern expression. And if she wasn't careful, she could lose her coveted position entirely. Then how would she pay her fall tuition? How would she live? And worse yet, she would earn a reputation for being a problem employee. If she wanted to become an FMO one day, she needed wildfire fighting experience. She didn't want to jeopardize her future career goals.

"You want my advice?" Jared asked.

No, but she realized he'd give it to her anyway. She nodded obediently, fearing what he might say.

"Suck it up. Get back to work and do your job. And next spring, if you still feel the same way, I'll put you at the top of the list for a move to another crew in Arizona or Montana."

A whoosh of air escaped Tessa's lungs. Arizona would be closer to Mom, but it'd be far away from Sean. That was good. It was what she wanted, after all. To get away from Sean.

"I doubt I'll be working on a hotshot crew next summer. I'll be graduating next spring and hopefully starting a new job in the Forest Service," she said.

He smiled wide. "That's right. I'd forgotten you were close to completing your schooling. Congratulations."

"Thank you."

"I hope you'll be able to finish out this summer here in Minoa. And after you graduate, maybe we can talk about your future. You've done a good job and I'd be happy to write you a letter of recommendation."

"Thank you. I'd like that very much," she said. She didn't want to jeopardize her opportunities by throwing a hissy fit now.

"So, do you think you're going to be okay to finish out the fire season?"

"Yes, I'll be fine. Thanks for talking with me about it," she said.

"You're welcome."

She fought off the urge to hand in her resignation right now. Instead, she kept her mouth shut by remembering her future plans and how blessed she was to be on this hotshot team.

"On a happier note, I've heard that Pete's gonna be okay," Jared said.

"Yes, he'll be fine. Sean did a good job handling the situation." And she meant every word. But she couldn't forget the anxiety she'd seen in his eyes, or how his breathing had come hard and fast as if he'd been running a marathon. Those symptoms weren't normal. What if Sean was suffering from PTSD? What if he needed help and didn't even know it?

"I'm glad to hear you say that," he said.

As she stood to leave, Tessa assessed her options. She would have to finish the season on the Minoa hotshot crew. She had to do it. She'd control her raging emotions, be quiet and do her job. And in the process, she must not let herself love Sean again. No, sirree. One broken heart was enough.

"Excuse me." Sean whipped around the corner of the FMO's office and almost fell over the top of a woman.

He'd been running late for his meeting with Jared Marshall and not paying attention. Lifting his hands, he drew back, but not before he caught the woman's sweet scent. A mingling of fragrant shampoo, delicate perfume and clean skin. Subtle and nice. And in that single moment of time, he recognized her even before he stared into her wide, uncertain eyes.

"Tessie." He whispered her name. Or at least he thought he did. He couldn't be sure, because the moment he saw her, his thoughts scattered like the wind tosses autumn leaves in October.

She flattened herself against the wall, her lips parted as she inhaled a shaky breath. She appeared as startled as he did. "Sean. I didn't expect to see you here."

Apparently not. A feeling of confusion zipped through his mind. He'd been working on reports in his office all afternoon and thought she was out in the repair shop with the other crew members back at the hotshot base. She must have asked her squad leader for some personal time off, which was perfectly fine. But...

"What are you doing here?" he said.

Maybe he shouldn't have asked that. It wasn't his business, after all. She was allowed to take personal leave to attend to her own affairs. But he was so taken off guard that the question slipped out before he could think to pull it back.

"Um, I had some business to tend to. I'm headed back to work right now." Her face brightened up like a flamethrower. Her gaze darted toward the front door, and she inched down the hallway. She obviously didn't like him finding her here.

"Okay, I won't keep you. See you later." He waved

her on, mildly amused by the rush of relief that relaxed her tensed shoulders.

She darted toward freedom. The moment she disappeared from view, he wished he'd said something different. Something gentle and encouraging to put her at ease. It was as if they were both lepers and feared catching the contagious disease from one another.

A nagging suspicion tugged at him. He couldn't help wondering why she was at the forest supervisor's office during work hours.

Swiveling on his boot heels, he knocked on Jared Marshall's office door.

"Enter."

He turned the knob and poked his head inside. "You ready for our meeting?"

Jared looked up and waved. "Yeah. Hi, Sean. Sit down. I understand that Pete's gonna be okay."

Sean entered the room and shut the door behind him. Reclining back in his seat, Jared indicated a hard-backed chair in front of his desk.

Reaching out, Sean handed over his incident report then sat and crossed his legs. "That's right. They'll release him from the hospital in a few days. But I don't think he'll be back on the fireline this season. It'll take him months to heal enough for active duty again."

Jared slapped the report on his desk but didn't flip through the pages. Sean knew the man would review it in detail once he left.

"I'm just glad he's going to recover. Can you hold his position open? Or do we need to replace him before next summer?" Jared asked.

"I'll be down three men for the rest of this season, but we can hold it open for now. Pete insists he wants to come back as soon as he's strong enough. I've assured him his position will be here when he's ready." Sean still couldn't believe Pete was willing to come back after what had happened. But no one had died, thankfully.

"Good." Jared nodded. "I understand you handled the situation with precision. You saved Pete's life."

Sean didn't see it that way. "I just did my job."

Jared snorted. "And pretty well, from what I've heard. Even Tessa said you saved Pete."

Sean hesitated, stunned by this news. "She actually said that?"

"Yeah, in those exact words. We talked for a few minutes."

"About what?" He had to know.

Jared arched one brow then filled him in on Tessa's request to be transferred to another hotshot crew.

Something cold gripped Sean's heart. He wanted her off the fireline so she would be safe, but if she transferred to a different crew, he wouldn't be able to keep his promise to Zach. He wouldn't be able to keep her safe. And that thought terrified him.

"You should tell her the truth, Sean," Jared said.

"And what's the truth?"

"That it was Zach's fault he died. He chose to run the other way. You couldn't stop him. It wasn't your fault. You did the right thing by fighting for your life," Jared said.

Sean didn't agree, but he knew he couldn't go on feeling this guilt and pain indefinitely. It was destroying him, eating him up inside. At some point he'd have to make a change. He just wasn't certain how to go about it. Maybe Tessa was right. Maybe he should try handing his burdens over to God.

"Are you still meeting regularly with your psychiatrist?" Jared asked.

"No, I finished my protocol." Sean had worked hard with a doctor to overcome his survivor's guilt but had never succeeded. He had gone through the motions and completed the program before Jared had agreed to let him back on the fireline. Thinking it a weakness, Sean had done his best to hide his PTSD symptoms. But they were still there. He didn't want to make a big deal about it. He just needed to get his fears under control. Surely his PTSD would go away in time. He didn't need anyone's help. Did he?

"You might consider a refresher course, just to keep yourself on an even keel. Your psychological well-being is as important as your physical health," Jared said.

"I'll think about it." But even as he said the words, Sean knew he wouldn't go back to the shrink. Talking about his problems with a strange doctor only made things worse. He wanted to forget what had happened, not rehash the horror again and again by talking about it.

"Well, good work. I'm pleased with how this recent fire turned out in spite of Pete getting hurt," Jared said.

"You and me both."

Jared leaned forward and met his eyes. "Now, what are you going to do about Tessa?"

Love her. Keep her safe. Until his dying breath.

"We won't have any problems. I'll make sure of that. We'll make it work," Sean said.

Jared sat back and released a deep breath. "Try to be as gentle with her as you can, but I don't want anything to compromise the well-being of the crew. If push comes to shove, I'm prepared to make a change. I can't just move her to another hotshot crew. I can give her a good reference, but she'd have to apply once an opening becomes available and the superintendent of that crew would have to agree to take her on."

Sean hesitated, knowing what this meant. If Tessa couldn't make her job here in Minoa work, she might not be able to get on another crew even if Jared pulled some strings. Sean didn't want Tessa to lose her job. "I understand. But I'm confident it will be okay."

"Good," Jared said.

As Jared addressed several other work issues, Sean forced himself to focus. To take notes and provide feedback. But when he left, he couldn't remember a word he'd said to Jared. His chest felt heavy as though a dark storm cloud had settled there.

For Tessa's benefit, he had to make their relationship on the hotshot team work. No matter what, he was determined to get along with her. He had to keep his promise to Zach. But that didn't mean he knew how to resolve this conflict between them. He thought again about giving the Lord a second chance. He'd try almost anything if it would ease the ache in his heart, but he sure didn't believe that prayer was the answer.

Chapter Eleven

The roar of chain saws filled Tessa's ears. Standing on the east side of the Sierra Nevadas, she gazed out at the rugged mountains covered with lush green alpine meadows and thick stands of pine trees. If her team didn't get the fireline built soon, all of this natural beauty would be consumed within a matter of hours.

It had been only a week since she'd asked the FMO to transfer her to another hotshot crew, yet it seemed more like years. Now another fire burned nearby, its warmth almost unbearable. The wind blew toward the team, pushing thick clouds of smoke in their direction. A whoosh of sound jerked Tessa around as a large, rotting log burst into flames like a lighted matchstick. The sudden heat blasted her face and she turned away from its intensity, closing her eyes.

Harlie yelled. He and Dean attacked the burning log, breaking up the fuel and shoveling dirt over it to snuff out the flames.

"Bump!" Sean called from nearby.

The order was passed down the row of crew members. Without question, the first man at the head of the line fell back while the rest of the crew adjusted their position forward. Taking turns in this process helped keep the lead person on the line from getting overly exhausted.

Sean stood a stone's throw away, a scowl pulling his brows together as he studied the fireline.

"Can you hear the river below us?" Tessa asked him, speaking over the jangling whine of saws.

He tilted his head in a quizzical frown. "No, it's not a river."

Well, it sounded like a river to her. Like the great rushing of a waterfall. But that couldn't be. She'd seen the waterway etched clearly on the map that the crew had studied before they began their work at two o'clock that morning. Surely they hadn't traveled that far north yet.

She caught the brief squawk of static. Looking up, she saw Sean speaking into the radio, his face stoic. He nodded, his lips moving as he replied in the affirmative. Something must be wrong.

"Stop work now! Move into that rocky clearing, pronto!" he bellowed to the crew and pointed to their right.

The safety zone!

Tessa and the rest of the crew didn't need to be told twice. Packing their hand tools with them, they all hustled across the clearing. Glancing over her shoulder, she saw Sean shepherding the team up the hill. He was the last man to make it to the safety zone, and it struck her that he was ensuring every member of the team arrived safely. As they all huddled among the boulders and blackened trees previously burned by the fire, Tessa realized it would be so easy for someone to fall behind and get lost in all the smoke.

Sean crouched close beside her. No doubt dispatch, or their lookout, had warned him of some impending danger. In spite of her desire to get away from him, she took comfort from his presence. With him near, she felt safe.

She studied the thick carpet of dried pine needles and half-burned trees covering the area. It'd be so easy for the wind to change direction and push the fire right over top of them in a reburn. They were secure for now, but that could change in a moment.

The growl of the river increased and Tessa realized her error. It wasn't a river at all, but a firestorm raging across the forest below them. The crashing and crackling increased to a fierce crescendo as the fire boiled up and consumed everything in its path. Choking billows of smoke filled the air, and she covered her nose and mouth. Soon the fire reached the area where the crew had been working just minutes earlier. In spite of the brutal heat, Tessa shivered, grateful that Sean had moved the team out of harm's way.

Blinking her dry eyes, she looked at him. He was crouched low, his long legs crammed against the rocks. He'd gotten them out of danger, but something in his eyes seemed so chilling. A mixture of anxiety and fear. Even though they were no longer running, his breathing was shallow. Like the day when Pete had been hurt. His eyes were wide as he stared at the fire with dread. Something was off-kilter. The other men were too far away to notice, but she did. And she wondered again if he was suffering from PTSD.

"Sean, are you okay?" she asked, knowing there was

no way the other men could overhear her above the roar of the fire.

He glanced at her and blinked his eyes as if coming back to the present. A trace of hesitancy flickered over his face. Then his jaw hardened and he looked away. "I'm fine. We'll all be fine."

What kind of answer was that? Something was definitely wrong. She'd never seen him like this before. He wasn't himself. In fact, she didn't recognize this man.

She leaned closer. "You don't need to worry about the team. We're all well trained and know how to take orders. Everything is going to be all right."

She wondered why she was reassuring him. After all, she wanted nothing to do with this man anymore. But an instinctive knowledge took hold of her. Something she couldn't deny. In her heart, she knew it was the right thing to do. Her intuition told her that he was in trouble. And no matter how badly he'd hurt her, he had once meant everything to her. She couldn't turn her back on him, not if he needed her help.

"It's going to be okay," she said.

He inhaled a shuddering breath, speaking softly, as if to himself. "If he had just stayed with me, he would have been okay."

She tensed. Had she heard him right? "What did you say?"

He shook his head and took a cleansing breath as if forcing himself to relax. "Nothing. Never mind."

No, surely she had heard him correctly. And he must be talking about Zach. His words were revealing, but what did they mean? She knew that her brother's body had been found down by Gosser's Creek, but Sean had taken refuge in a previously burned area where he had deployed his fire shelter. The two men had obviously gotten separated. But was that because Sean had abandoned Zach? Or was it because Zach couldn't or wouldn't stay with Sean? And why? What had happened?

She scooted nearer, sitting no more than a hand's breadth away from him, grateful for the sounds of the burnover to mask their conversation. "Sean, we used to confide in one another. Do you want to talk about it? Maybe I can help."

His eyes widened with surprise. He opened his mouth as if he wanted to speak but then shook his head as though he'd changed his mind. "No, it's all right. You can't help me. No one can."

His words pinched her heart, confirming her fear that he was struggling right now. But she had no idea what to do. "The Lord can help. He's always there for each one of us, and He will never betray a confidence. But sometimes He waits for us to seek Him out."

Sean's eyes narrowed with anger. "God didn't answer my prayers the day Zach died. I doubt He'd answer them now."

He swiveled around, showing her his back, cutting off further conversation. She gaped at him in astonishment, catching a glimpse of what it must have been like for him when he lost Zach. She remembered her conversation with Jared and a thought occurred to her. What if Sean had pushed her away not because of anything he had done, but because of what he could not do? He couldn't save her brother, but he had saved himself. And maybe that was the crux of the problem. Maybe he felt guilty for living, for surviving, when Zach had perished. For whatever reason, Zach had not stayed with him. He hadn't made it to the safety zone. Which wouldn't have been Sean's fault. Or was it?

Long minutes passed. The wind picked up and a rush of hot air blasted Tessa. She took a deep inhale against her shirtsleeve, shielding her lungs from the burning fumes. Waves of ash and glowing embers floated over top of the crew. She watched as Harlie pulled a granola bar out of his web belt and chewed furiously. Tessa knew eating at a time like this was a release of nervous energy.

An hour later Sean's radio crackled with static. He talked to home base for a few moments then called the team back to work.

"The fire has passed us by. Line out, but stay vigilant," he said.

Tessa stood on wobbly legs, her back stiff, her feet rolling against loose gravel and rocks. Someone grabbed her arm to steady her and she looked up into Sean's eyes.

"I'd hate to have you ride out a burnover only to tumble down this mountainside," he said, his mouth curved in a half smile.

She froze, gazing up at him. Trying to see the truth in his eyes. His doubt and anguish appeared to be gone, replaced by the confident man she'd known for so long. He seemed his regular self again with no signs of PTSD.

"Thanks." Her voice sounded vague and she watched as he turned and stepped away.

She followed him back to the fireline they'd been building among the heavy stand of timber. Overhead she caught the low murmur of a plane. Simultaneously, the crew members turned their faces skyward as a big Sikorsky helicopter roared above them. The chopper's hammering staccato seemed to vibrate through Tessa's bones.

The chopper lowered over the sway of giant pine trees, zipping straight toward the hotshot crew. Tessa had seen this layout many times but never up this close and personal.

"Oh, no. Tell me he's not gonna dump that retardant on top of us," Tank said with disbelief.

"Look out! We're about to get drenched," Sean yelled the warning.

Poof!

A long, red cloud of fire retardant streamed from the underbelly of the aircraft, bearing down on Tessa. She stared in horror. Her mouth dropped open and she felt as though her feet were nailed to the ground. Unable to move. Like the big chopper was about to gobble her up.

"Tessa, get down!"

She found herself knocked back beneath the cover of tree limbs. A heavy weight rested over the top of her, shielding her from the shower of fire retardant. She lay with her face pressed into the dirt, the caustic scent of ammonia burning her nostrils. After a moment, the heavy weight lifted off her and she pushed herself up, staring at Sean. She felt dazed and shocked, trying to shake it off. Confused by her own failure to act, she blinked at him.

"What were you doing?" He spoke in a deep voice roughened by emotion.

She felt locked there. Suspended in time. A shiver swept down her spine, but she couldn't turn her face away. In that brief moment, she remembered each and every time this man had touched her.

"I... I didn't think," she murmured, wondering what

was wrong with her. She'd never frozen up like that before. For just a few critical moments she'd panicked and felt stapled in place. Unable to think. Unable to move.

The noxious retardant was a mixed blessing. It snuffed out burning embers and decelerated the fire, but it had also coated the crew members in red, slimy muck.

Everyone except her. Thanks to Sean. Once again he'd come to her aid. Always there. Always keeping her safe.

He held out a hand to help her regain her feet but she ignored it, standing on her own. "You don't need to do that."

"Do what?" he asked.

"Protect me all the time."

"Why didn't you duck?" he asked.

"I was so surprised, I didn't think to react fast enough."

"You know you can't lose your nerve like that on the fireline. You have to act fast," he said.

Yes, she knew. But she'd just learned that saying it and doing it were two different things.

"I wish you wouldn't show me any preferential treatment." She spoke in a low tone so the other men wouldn't hear.

"What do you mean?" Sean asked.

"I can do my job just fine."

"I know that. I didn't do anything for you that I wouldn't have done for one of the men." His jaw looked hard as granite.

"Is that right? You would have tackled Tank and knocked him out of the way?" she challenged.

His jaw tightened. "Yes, if necessary."

He stepped back, looking embarrassed and confused.

A barrage of laughter sounded behind her as the men swiped at their saturated clothes. Tessa decided that if it was a choice between burning to death or being covered by fire retardant, she'd take the Sikorsky every time. But losing it the way she'd done had confused her. She'd never fallen apart like that and pondered how it might feel to face a wall of flame with no escape route at her back.

Was that how it had been for Zach and Sean? Nowhere to go. No way to flee. She couldn't imagine Sean freezing up like she had done, but what about Zach? Jared had mentioned it, as well. Was that why her brother hadn't been found with Sean? Had he panicked?

Taking advantage of the retardant, the crew members attacked the spot fires. They laughed and joked as they worked.

"Tessa's the only member of the crew who didn't get covered in slimy muck," Ace said in a jovial tone. "She shouldn't need to clean up much when we get off the fireline."

Looking down at her filthy clothes, Tessa knew she was black with soot and stank of smoke. Except for the fire retardant, she was just as filthy as the men.

"Yeah, right. I almost look like I'm ready for the prom," she said with a good-natured laugh.

She chopped and scraped with her Pulaski as though this was an everyday occurrence. No big deal. But inside she was muddled. A knot of apprehension tightened at the back of her neck.

She thought about all the times when Sean had kept her safe. Maybe she was viewing this all wrong. Instead of his unwanted attention being a nuisance, maybe it was a revelation into his true feelings toward her. That he still cared for her. And if she was honest with herself, she still cared for him, too. Although she feared Sean was suffering from PTSD and survivor's guilt, she knew she couldn't make him love her if he didn't want to. But was his guilt reason enough for him to break up with her? Maybe he was innocent of doing anything wrong, but he still felt responsible. If so, what could she do about it? She didn't have a clue how to help him get past it.

Sean turned away from Tessa, forcing himself to get back to work. To concentrate on his job. But his hands were shaking and he gripped his Pulaski harder as he scraped the ground. Bending over the thick root of a waxy currant bush, he resisted the harsh memories that pulsed over him in crashing waves. Memories of him calling to Zach, begging him to stay with him. Not to run away. To come back and go with him to the safety zone. Sean had screamed Zach's name over and over until his voice was hoarse and the walls of flame had shut him off from view.

During the burnover, Tessa had reassured him. With her soft voice nearby, he'd felt a quiet peace envelop him. He was supposed to be watching over her, not the other way around. She'd been sympathetic when she didn't need to be, and that surprised him. He didn't deserve her kindness, but he appreciated it more than he could say. She'd asked him to confide in her, but talking about it would only make things worse. Wouldn't it?

"You got us through that burnover just fine, super," Tank said nearby. "Are you doing okay?"

Sean glanced at the man, noticing that Harlie had stopped to look at him, too. "Yeah, I'm fine."

Sean's face felt drained of color. In spite of his best efforts, his men must still be able to sense his unease. He was working extra hard because of Zach. They all remembered that horrible day and none of them wanted a repeat. But the last thing Sean wanted was for them to know that he was suffering from PTSD.

He expected the two men to move on, but they both remained by his side. They worked companionably for several moments as though they were offering him their silent support. Then Tank looked straight at him.

"You know it wasn't your fault, don't you, super?" Tank asked.

Sean paused, gripping the hickory handle of his Pulaski like a lifeline. "What wasn't my fault?"

"Last summer, when that big firestorm hit us and we lost Zach," Tank said. "What happened wasn't your fault. I just wanted you to know that's how I see it."

Harlie nodded in agreement. "That's right. I feel the same way, boss. It's time to let it go."

Sean's brain stumbled to a halt. Was he so transparent? For some crazy reason, hearing these words of support from members of his crew eased his mind a bit. But how could he let it go? There were some things a man just couldn't get over. Weren't there?

And then something amazing occurred to him. Maybe his crew didn't blame him for what had happened to Zach. Maybe Tessa didn't blame him, either. And if they could forgive him for not saving Zach, then maybe God could, too. He wouldn't know unless he finally asked the Lord. But that was only half the battle. Sean still didn't know if he could forgive himself.

Chapter Twelve

Tessa whisked the cream of chicken soup with a can of water then poured the mixture over the rice and chicken. Opening an envelope of onion soup mix, she sprinkled it over the top of everything. She then ripped off a sheet of tin foil and wrapped it over the glass baking pan before sliding it into the hot oven. After two weeks straight on the fireline, she wanted a home-cooked meal.

As she set the timer, she glared at her double kitchen sinks. It figured that one of them was clogged. The right side was running clear, but the left side with the garbage disposal in it had been blocked since early that morning. Because she didn't have the right tools, she hadn't been able to stop and fix it before she had left for work. She was planning to do that now, while her dinner baked.

To clear the blockage, she'd tried a plunger first but made the mistake of not covering the drain of the right sink. The moment she plunged the clogged sink, a geyser of murky water had shot up from the clear side and doused her in the process. She was getting ready to remove the contents of the cupboard so that she could have room to disassemble the pipes when the door-bell rang.

Pushing a strand of damp hair behind her ear, she padded across the living room in her bare feet. "Har-lie, it's about time you showed up. I hope you brought some channel locks. The joints on the pipes are tied to-gether pretty tight and I—" She gasped as she opened the door and stared in confusion. "Sean!"

"Hi, there."

He didn't smile. He stood in front of her, still wear-ing his hotshot uniform and holding a bright red tool-box in one hand. He must have just gotten off work, staying late to catch up on some paperwork or other administrative issues.

"What are you doing here?" she asked, trying not to sound annoyed. His timing couldn't be worse.

He showed a half smile, but it didn't quite reach his eyes. "I came to help with your plumbing problem."

She glanced behind him at the stairwell. "But where's Harlie? He promised to come over and help. I need his channel locks."

Sean lifted the toolbox. "I've got some. He sent me instead."

Tilting her head to one side, she frowned. That morn-ing she'd told Harlie about her clogged sink and he'd offered to come over right after work. She didn't really need his help, but she could sure use his tools.

"Why would he do that?" she asked.

Sean stepped past her into the tiny living room with-out being invited. She was forced to move back to give him room.

"He sends his apologies. He can't make it because he had to help his mom instead," he said.

Tessa closed the door then lifted a hand to rest on her hip. Suspicion fogged her brain. What was Harlie up to by sending Sean over here?

"Help his mom do what?" she asked.

Sean walked into the kitchen, his gaze whipping over to where she had set the table for two. She'd planned to feed Harlie supper, but Sean was a game changer. She wasn't prepared to share her meal with her ex-fiancé.

He set the toolbox on the counter next to the sinks. "Apparently her dog got out, so she called Harlie to help her find the animal."

Her eyes widened. "You mean that giant mastiff that got arrested for chasing livestock last year?"

The dog was huge and loved to chase cattle. Harlie's mom had been fined a couple of times before. One more offence and animal control had warned her that they would have to put the animal down.

Sean nodded. "The same. Knowing he couldn't come over here, Harlie asked me to do it."

Okay, she would forgive Harlie this time. She hated for his mom to lose her dog.

"You don't need to fix my clog," she said. "If I can just borrow some of your tools, I'll take care of it myself."

"I know you're capable of handling it, Tessa. I just came over to help." He lifted his face and breathed in deeply. "Are you cooking something?"

"Yes, chicken and rice casserole," she said.

Which happened to be one of Sean's favorites. She hadn't made the recipe in ages for that exact reason. Now he'd probably ask for an invitation.

But he didn't. Instead, he flipped open the metal

toolbox then studied the two inches of standing water in her sink.

"Have you tried plunging it yet?" he asked without looking up.

She chuckled and indicated her damp hair. "Oh, yes. Unfortunately, it didn't help."

As he looked at her, his lips twitched as though he was trying not to laugh. Tessa felt a flush of heat suffuse her face.

"Have you got a couple of towels and a bucket I can use?" he asked.

"Sure."

She walked down the hallway and retrieved the towels and mop bucket from the bathroom then returned. She found him removing all of the cleaning items and other junk she'd stashed beneath the sink and setting it aside so he could better access the pipes. Once he'd cleared an opening, he laid one towel inside the cupboard and placed the other towel close by, in case he needed it to sop up water. He then set the bucket beneath the pipes.

"Can we bail out some of the water in the sink?" he asked.

"Yes, of course." She moved into action. Retrieving a plastic cup from the cabinet, she dipped water over to the sink that still drained well. It took only a couple of minutes. When she'd sieved off as much of the excess water as she could, she looked up and found him watching her intently.

"What?" she asked.

A wry smile creased the corners of his mouth. He gestured to the cup she'd been using. "I like your frilly little cup."

Tessa glanced down and gave a small groan. She'd grabbed the first thing that had met her fingers. Her bright pink princess cup. It was old and scratched and slightly warped from the heat of the dishwasher, but she couldn't bring herself to part with it.

"Zach bought it for me when he went to Disneyland with his football team in high school," she said.

He arched one brow, looking quizzical. "A princess cup? It doesn't seem to suit you."

She shrugged, unable to prevent an embarrassed smile. "Not now, but it did in those days. I was very into princesses as a little girl."

She didn't mention how she'd daydreamed that her prince charming would one day come and carry her off into the sunset. With her father leaving when she was so young, she'd always hoped she might find someone to love. And when she did, it hadn't ended well.

He smiled. "I can believe that. You know how to fight fire with the men, but there's a gentle, feminine side to you, as well. You dress up real nice."

The compliment startled her and a warm, pleasant feeling swept over her. She liked that he knew that about her. In fact, maybe they knew a bit too much about each other. Which reminded her that she was longing to ask him about his PTSD. Because frankly, she was worried about him. And for some crazy reason worrying about him made her forget her own anger and pain. It made her want to help him.

"Let me take a look at this clog." He got down on the floor and shimmied into the cabinet. Lying on his back, he looked up at the pipes.

Tessa crouched at his feet, peering in at what he was

doing. "I've already tried to loosen the joints, but they wouldn't budge."

He reached up and gripped one pipe, trying to loosen it with his bare hands. He gave a low grunt. "You're right. They're really snug. Can you hand me the channel locks?" His voice sounded slightly muffled.

She rummaged around in his toolbox and retrieved the tool then handed it to him. Within moments he had the joints loosened. A slow trickle of water dripped down onto his face and he blinked, moving his head to the side.

"Can you hand me the bucket?" he asked.

She did so and he placed it on his chest, letting the water drizzle into the container. Tessa saw that he was holding the P-trap steady, patiently waiting for it to drain a little bit before he opened it up. He then removed the tube and looked inside.

"Oh, yes. Here's the problem." He tilted it so she could see the potato peelings, egg shells and black sludge clogging the pipe.

"Yuck," she said. "Did I do that?"

He tapped the pipe against the bucket and the clog popped right out. He chuckled. "You must have, unless you've got someone sneaking into your house and clogging your sink when you're not at home."

She laughed and it felt good. So comfortable. So natural. They'd been sad for so long. Maybe too long.

"Yeah, that's what it must have been. Someone sneaking into my house," she said.

"But seriously, potato peelings go through the garbage disposal a whole lot easier if you put them in that side of the sink," he said. "They don't go down the regular drain very well."

She felt a flush of embarrassment suffuse her face. "I'm usually careful about it, but I guess some of the peelings got into the wrong sink."

"It's a common mistake." He shifted his long legs so he could put the P-trap back into place.

Tessa backed up to give him more room to work. She knew she could have cleaned out the clog, but having him here made her strangely content and happy inside. And for a few moments she wondered where those feelings came from.

The timer went off and she quickly opened the oven door so she could peer inside at her casserole. A blast of warmth struck her in the face. Ten more minutes and dinner would be ready. She could hear Sean rummaging around the pipes beneath her sinks.

"Let's check the garbage disposal while I'm down here. I'll have you turn it and the water on." He paused for a moment. "But not quite yet."

Too late. She'd already switched on the disposal and turned the tap on full boar, so she lunged to turn everything off. But not before water spewed out from beneath the cabinet.

"Whoa!" he yelled.

Thud!

His legs jerked and she knew he must have hit his forehead on the pipes above him. His hands dropped to his sides and he lay very still.

"Sean!" She knelt beside him and leaned into the cabinet.

His eyes were closed. A red goose egg was forming on his forehead.

Leaning near, she patted his cheek. "Sean, are you okay?"

He opened his eyes and looked up at her, their noses almost touching. Lifting his hand, he rubbed the bump gently. "Ouch! That hurt."

"Did I knock you out?"

"No, I was just stunned for a moment. I wasn't expecting to get soaked like that."

He was okay. What a relief. She reached for the extra towel and wiped the water off his face. "I'm so sorry. I didn't mean for you to get hurt."

He gazed into her eyes. So close that she could feel his breath whisper past her cheek. Warning bells chimed inside her head, but she ignored them. He looked as startled as she felt. She longed to forget all the sadness between them. She wanted to comfort him. To make him happy. To see him smile and laugh again.

A dubious frown pulled his eyebrows together. "Tell me you didn't do that on purpose."

She laughed. "Okay. I didn't do that on purpose... or did I?"

She didn't know why she was teasing him. The words just seemed to come out.

A smile widened his handsome mouth. "Next time I'll let you clean out the clog and I'll turn on the water."

"Deal. There isn't much you and I can't do together," she said.

His smile evaporated, and his eyes filled with so much sadness that she wanted to cry. She realized that her hand rested lightly against his chest. She could feel the rapid beating of his heart beneath her fingers. Her common sense told her to pull away now. Being this close to him was dangerous to her heart. But his gaze was mesmerizing, drawing her closer like a magnetic pull. His sorrow reached out and slowly reeled her in like a fish on a line.

She kissed him. Or he kissed her. She wasn't sure which. Softly. A gentle caress as she breathed deeply of his spicy scent. All that mattered in that moment of time was Sean. His pain. His hopes and dreams. Helping him heal enough that he could finally talk about what had happened to him. And then she would need the courage to accept whatever he told her.

He shifted closer to her. She could feel his fingers twining through her long hair. Could feel the soft warmth of his lips against her own. And then he pushed her away.

"No, Tessa. I can't. It won't work." A shudder trembled over him and he quickly scooted out from beneath the cabinet so he could stand.

Tessa's face heated up like road flares. She felt scalded. Like she was a naughty little child. Embarrassed and hurt.

She stood up, too, and turned away, her mind swirling with emotions she couldn't understand. She felt confused and humiliated.

They didn't look at each other and she made a pretense of checking the oven again. Trying to pretend the kiss never happened. Trying to regain the resentment she'd felt toward him when she'd first returned to town. To keep blaming him for Zach's death. But somehow she just didn't feel that way anymore. Anger wouldn't bring her brother back, nor would it help her or Sean to heal from their loss. Now all that remained was the aching sting of Sean's rejection. And being close to Sean like this would only make it worse. But maybe he shouldn't have broken up with her. And she wondered if he might regret it, just a teensy bit.

He raked his fingers through his hair. "How do you cope?"

His question stunned her. "With what?"

"The loss. Missing Zach."

Wow! This was a first. She didn't expect such queries from him. And maybe it was good that he'd asked. It opened the door to some of the questions pounding her mind.

Sean waited for Tessa's response. A part of him knew her answer already, but another part of him wanted to hear it one more time.

"I've coped because the Lord has carried me through," she said. "It hasn't been easy, but I know He's been there with me through it all. He's made the loss more bearable."

He snorted and rummaged around in his toolbox, pretending to look for another tool. He knew he was giving her the cold shoulder again, but he couldn't help it. She made prayer sound so easy. But it wasn't. Not for him. And that was when he realized that he didn't want to talk to God. He didn't want to hand his grief over to the Lord. Because then he'd be free of the guilt. And he didn't think he deserved that kind of peace. He didn't deserve to be happy again. Or did he?

"Sean, I think you're suffering from PTSD. And if that's true, then you need help." Tessa touched his arm, looking up at him with compassion in her eyes.

He jerked his head toward her, trying not to let her see how he was feeling inside. The last thing he wanted was her pity.

"I don't have PTSD," he said. But he knew that he did. He'd pushed it aside, ignoring the problem. He was strong, after all. He could handle anything. He just needed time. Didn't he?

Her lips tightened. "You act like you do."

He paused, knowing that he was in denial. He had tried so hard, but maybe he couldn't deal with his PTSD on his own. The anxiety attacks, the insomnia, the flashbacks to the day of the fire. Surely he would get over it soon. Then again, maybe not. It had already been almost a year and nothing had improved for him. Maybe he did need help after all.

She dropped her hand away, her eyes filled with doubt. "I think you need to talk about it with someone."

"Who did you have in mind?" he asked.

"I was always a good listener. We used to tell each other everything."

"You wouldn't like what you hear this time," he said.

Her jaw tightened as if she was trying to be brave. "Why don't you try me?"

No, he couldn't do that. He couldn't tell her all of those horrible things. He wanted to protect her. He didn't want to fill her mind with visions of death.

"Maybe another time," he said.

"Then if you won't talk to me, please talk to someone else, Sean. You seem so unhappy. You're not yourself anymore. I think talking about it is the only way you can ever get feeling better."

Ah, she knew him so well. He didn't bother to ask how she knew he was depressed. He'd tried so hard to hide it. But he'd never been able to keep anything from Tessa. And this weakness emasculated him like nothing else could.

"I need to finish up here and get going." Brushing past her, he reached under the sink and dried off the pipes then ensured that the joints were all tight.

"Can you turn on the water? I want to check one last time for leaks," he said.

She released a sigh of disappointment but did as asked. The rush of water filled the sink as she turned on the tap. He studied the pipes, remembering the kiss they'd shared a few minutes earlier. It had been a serious lapse of judgment for him to have allowed that to happen. Because now he only wanted more. And he couldn't have Tessa. Not as long as he blamed himself for Zach's death. Not without wondering every moment that they were together if she blamed him, too, but was just putting on a good front. Unless she absolutely believed in him, her doubts would canker inside her and eventually blow up. Their relationship would be doomed to failure.

"Everything looks good," he said.

"Wonderful. Thank you for all your help," she said, her voice sounding tight.

"My pleasure." And he meant it. He wanted to help her. Because of what she had once meant to him. Because of what she still meant to him.

"Will you stay for supper? It's all ready. I've got a salad in the fridge and rocky road ice cream for dessert," she said.

She folded her arms and stepped back while he retrieved his channel locks. He returned them to his toolbox then closed and latched the lid. His stomach rumbled and the casserole smelled good enough to tempt him, but it would be a mistake to stay. Because he might lose his willpower. It was better not to torture either of them with any false hopes.

"Thanks, but I better get going. I've got some reports to finish for the FMO by tomorrow morning. If we get called out on another fire and I'm not prepared, he won't be happy with me." It was the truth, after all.

"Are you sure? Even if you have reports to fill out, you still have to eat," she said.

"No, but thanks anyway."

There. He'd been strong. It was the best thing to do.

He stepped outside and she followed him, leaning against the doorjamb.

"See you tomorrow," she said.

"Yeah, tomorrow." He waved and walked to the parking lot. He forced himself not to look back, although he wanted to.

Placing his toolbox in the back of his truck, he then climbed into the driver's seat. He gripped the steering wheel with both hands and gazed up at Tessa's apartment on the second floor. She'd gone back inside and closed the door.

He couldn't believe he'd kissed her. Or she'd kissed him. He wasn't sure which. He had to be stronger than that. And he mustn't let it ever happen again.

Chapter Thirteen

The following morning Tessa ran along a steep, rocky path in the low hills surrounding the hotshot base. The crisp morning air invigorated her. Warm sunlight glinted off the white stones edging the trail, momentarily blinding her. She blinked and continued on.

"Come on! Pick up the pace," Sean yelled as he stood at the side of the trail and waited for the crew to jog past him.

He fell in behind Ace, silently urging the man to move a little faster. It wasn't easy to hike up a vertical incline while carrying a forty-five-pound pack on your back. Not at this pace. But it was Sean's responsibility to keep his team in optimal condition. Tessa silently admitted that he'd done an outstanding job as their superintendent. She now knew that he was the best man for the job and that she'd misjudged him. If only she could help him see that.

"Oww!" A hollow cry of pain wrenched from her throat as she stumbled and rolled into the thick clumps of rabbit brush lying a few feet off the trail. Curled on the ground, she pulled her right ankle close to her chest, hugging it tight.

Great! Just great. She hadn't been paying attention and may have injured herself pretty bad.

Several of the men hurried after her, crowding around as she grimaced in agony.

"Let me through." Sean elbowed his way past the guys. "Hey, you okay?" he asked, going down on one knee beside her.

She recoiled, fearing he might touch her. Fearing that she'd fall into his arms if he did. Through a fog of pain, she saw the fear etching his features. She had no doubt that it was genuine.

"I'm fine," she gasped.

But she wasn't. She didn't want to be a baby, but the throbbing in her ankle brought a sting of tears to her eyes. She clenched them shut, fighting off the pain.

"What happened?" he asked.

"A rock rolled beneath my foot." No way was she going to tell him that she'd been thinking about him and not paying attention to the uneven ground.

Thankfully, Harlie slipped the heavy backpack off her shoulders. As he swept it out of the way, she lay back to catch her breath.

"Just give me a moment and I'll be up again." She spoke the words through gritted teeth.

"You gonna be okay?" Sean asked.

She slit her eyes open to look at him. "Of course. It's nothing. I'll be fine."

But even as she said the words, she knew she was in trouble. She just hoped it wasn't serious.

He rolled up her pant leg to inspect the injury. His fingers were warm and gentle as he unlaced her boot and lowered her thick stocking for a better look. She wanted to push him away but couldn't resist feeling grateful that he was there. She could no longer fight him. Now she just wanted to help him.

"Ouch!" she cried.

"I don't think you're going to be hiking anymore today. Your ankle is swelling right before my eyes." He cupped her foot, gently testing the soundness of the bones.

Oh, no. That was not what she wanted to hear right now.

"Look at that, dudes. Hot pink nail polish. I'll bet Tessa could really rock a pair of high heels." Ace laughed and pointed at her painted toes.

"Knock it off." Sean growled the reprimand without looking up.

Ace shut his mouth, but the guys all stared at her foot. As the only woman on the team, Tessa was a novelty and they'd never stop teasing her about it. She knew Ace was joking to relieve a tense situation. She just hoped she wasn't going to be laid up with a broken ankle that prohibited her from fighting any more fires this season. She needed her paycheck.

She took several shallow breaths. "I couldn't catch myself in time and down I went."

"You could have a hairline fracture. I think you're gonna need some X-rays," Sean said.

No! She couldn't give in. She reached for her stocking to tug it back on. "I'll be okay. Let me get my boot back on and…oww!"

She dropped the shoe, her futile attempts at bravery forgotten for now.

"Get this out of here." Sean tossed the boot to Harlie, who whisked it behind his back.

"Hey! Give me that," she cried.

Sean showed a stern expression. "Tessa, your hike is finished for today."

She scowled, and no one asked why. If she couldn't walk, she couldn't fight wildfire. No doubt Sean was delighted to have her off the fireline. The day Pete was injured, Sean had been delighted to send her away. But she had to think about this rationally. The price she'd pay for taking this tumble could be steep. But it couldn't be helped now.

"We're gonna put you in the truck and take you to the clinic for some X-rays," he reiterated.

"No. Please. Just get me back to base and let me rest for the day. I'll be fine in the morning." She tried to stand, gave a low moan and sank back into the dirt. She was not going to be able to work today and she knew it.

Sean stood and nodded at the men. "Okay, guys, you know what to do. Let's get her back to base camp."

Tessa released a disgruntled groan but didn't fight them as Tank and Dean pulled her up. Bending her knee, she kept her injured foot from touching the ground. She looped her arms around the two men's necks and let them help her limp down the hill and back to the hotshot base. It was slow going until they got onto the flat trail at the bottom of the hill. By that time, Tessa was gritting her teeth in agony. She hoped it was just a sprain but, if it was, it was a doozy.

As they loaded Tessa into the supray, Sean gave several orders to the men. She knew they would continue with their workout while Sean drove her to the clinic in town.

Inside the truck neither Sean nor Tessa spoke until they arrived. She couldn't help thinking about the kiss they'd shared the day before. Surely it hadn't meant anything. Just a natural reflex from when they'd been happy and in love. The heat of the moment. But what if it was something more? She didn't know how to be sure. And then another thought occurred to her. What if Sean still loved her? What if breaking up with her had been all wrong? She wasn't sure if she wanted him back or not. Right now she didn't know how she felt about this man. If she let down her defenses, she could find herself hurt even worse. And yet a part of her wanted to try one more time.

He walked around to her door, opened it and scooped her into his arms to carry her inside. His touch seemed to almost burn her.

"Put me down. I can walk on my own," she demanded.

He kept walking, seeming to carry her as easily as he would a sack of feathers. Mortification burned her skin. She gave him her fiercest glare but he just stared straight ahead. She wanted to walk and he wouldn't let her. It was that simple. And he was big enough and strong enough that she couldn't fight him.

"What are you gonna do, crawl into the emergency room?" he asked, a twinge of humor tainting his words.

The vision of her crawling across the asphalt made her laugh. "No, of course not. But you've got to stop babying me, Sean."

"I'm not babying you," he insisted.

"Yes, you are. You wouldn't carry Harlie or Dean if one of them hurt their ankle. You would have gone for a wheelchair," she said.

He grunted, his eyebrows curved in a deep glower. "Waiting for a wheelchair would take too long."

The double automatic doors at the entrance whooshed open and he stepped inside. Numerous people sat in the waiting room, their gazes pinned on her.

"Everyone is staring at me," she whispered.

"That's because they know you're hurt. It's normal curiosity, nothing more," he said.

Well, yeah, but she didn't want to draw attention to herself. She was used to being strong and carrying her own load. They were hotshots. She was supposed to take care of people, not the other way around. It didn't sit well with her to rely on Sean's strength right now.

"Maybe you ought to admit that you can't do everything alone," he said. "It's okay to need other people once in a while. You should accept their help and say thank you."

"Back at you, buddy," she said. "You should take some of your own advice."

His jaw hardened but he didn't reply. Which was the most maddening character trait he had. When she wanted to have a good, loud argument, he just shut his mouth tight and wouldn't say a word.

As he trudged with her over to a chair, she finally gave it up and looped her hands around his neck to hold on. The feel of his arms around her did something to Tessa. It reminded her of happier days. A time when they didn't know how hurt they both could be.

"I mean it, Sean. You need help, too. You shouldn't push people away," she said.

"Let's not talk about this right now. We're here for you, not me." He bent over and gently deposited her in a seat.

"Why do you keep shutting me out? You need me. Is it so hard for you to admit it?"

He jerked his head up and met her eyes. Maybe she shouldn't have said that, but lately she'd been thinking it was true. That maybe it had been a mistake for her to let him break up with her. She was now convinced it never should have happened. But getting past his bull-headed stubbornness was another issue. Especially if he had PTSD. That wasn't something Sean would be able to just snap his fingers and push aside.

He heaved a disgruntled sigh. "You're relentless, did you know that? You never know when to quit."

He barely spared a glance at the busy waiting room before sauntering over to the front desk to speak with the receptionist. Before long, Tessa found herself in an examination room. Sean stayed with her the entire time as she was moved into the X-ray room then sent on her way home with an ice pack and a pair of crutches. A severe sprain, the doctor had said. Nothing broken. No ripped tendons. She should be feeling better in a week or two.

"Now watch. You and the guys will get called out on a fire and I'll be left behind," she grouched as Sean drove her home.

He chuckled, focusing his gaze on the windshield as he skirted through traffic. "Don't worry about that. Let's just get your ankle healed up."

She accepted that with a low sigh of impatience. Due to the fact that her injury wasn't serious and she also had a pain pill in her, she was feeling relaxed and mellow right now. Lethargic and easygoing.

"How's Matt doing?" she asked about the boy.

"Good. He's coming over later tonight. His mom has to work late and I promised to help him with his driving hours. But I might have to cancel and bring you some dinner instead."

"Absolutely not. I can take care of myself." But she knew if Sean was determined to bring her a meal, he'd do it no matter what she said. Of course, the meal would entail something from Megan's diner. There were no fast food restaurants in town and Sean didn't cook much, except for barbecuing steaks on the grill. But it was the thought that counted. He was always the caregiver. Always looking after everyone on the crew.

She arched her eyebrows. "Driving hours?"

"Yeah, Matt has to spend quite a few hours driving before he can qualify for his license. I've been teaching him."

"Zach taught me to drive." She smiled, the memory bringing her joy. And she recognized that it was getting easier to talk about her brother.

Sean chuckled. "I know. He told me what a crazy driver you were. It's a good thing he set you straight."

She reached across the seat and batted his shoulder playfully, feeling languid. "I'm a good driver."

"Yeah, sure you are. Now."

They both laughed…and then they went very still. Tessa blinked in confusion. For a few brief moments they'd both forgotten about the past. And Tessa thought now might be a good time to ask him once more about her brother. But knowing the truth didn't seem to be so important now. It occurred to her that, if she really believed in the atonement of Christ, then she needed to forgive Sean for whatever lapse in judgment he might have had that day. His guilt was unjustified and pre-

venting him from being able to feel the Savior's aton-
ing love. And that was when she realized the awesome
power she held. The power to keep Sean feeling guilty
and ugly inside, or to help him heal and feel joy. She
had to let the past go. To move on and remember Zach
with joy and love. Sean needed to do the same.

In her heart of hearts, she didn't believe he was responsible. Her brother's death was a terrible tragedy,
but it would be a complete disaster to lose Sean, too.
Not a physical death, but an emotional and spiritual one.
And she had to convince him of this.

But she couldn't think about it right now. She felt
dizzy, the pain pill making it difficult to concentrate.
Tomorrow. Tomorrow she'd talk to him. Somehow she
would find a way to get through to him. Because, no
matter what, she was not going to let him push her
away again.

Sean's cell phone rang. Because he was driving, he
tossed it over to Tessa. She punched a button and answered the call.

"Hullo. This is Tess." Her words sounded slightly
slurred and Sean glanced over at her.

She paused, listening. She mouthed Harlie's name so
that Sean knew who she was speaking with.

"Hi, Tessa. You doing okay?" Harlie asked.

"Yeah, I'm fine. Just a bad sprain. I've got to let the
tendons heal for a few days. What are you up to?"

She stifled a wide yawn, hardly able to keep her
eyes open. Sean shook his head, his brow creased in a
questioning frown.

"We've got a fire in Colorado," Harlie said.

Tessa's eyes popped open and she was now wide

awake. She repeated the words out loud for Sean's benefit. "You have a fire in Colorado?"

"Yes. Any idea when the super will be back at the base?" Harlie asked.

"He's dropping me off at my place right now and then he'll be coming in."

Sean nodded his approval. "Ask him to get my fire pack out, will you?"

She repeated the message into the phone, forcing herself to speak clearly.

"Will do," Harlie said. "And Tessa, get feeling better soon."

"Thanks, I will."

Sean turned the corner as she clicked off the phone and tossed it onto the seat between them.

"See? I told you that you'd get called out on a fire the very same day I get crippled," she grumbled.

He smiled. "It could be worse. At least nothing's broken. You'll be back fighting fire with us soon enough. Besides, I think you're gonna sleep for the rest of the day."

She grumbled under her breath, not liking this situation at all.

"Actually this is good timing," he said in a cheerful tone. "You'll be on desk duty until we get back. Hopefully it won't be long and your ankle will be better by the time we return."

"Uh-huh. You don't have to be so happy about it. I don't like the way you coddle me all the time. You almost act glad that I can't go on the fire with you." She folded her arms and closed her eyes, waiting for him to deny her accusation. But she didn't hear him speak until they arrived at her apartment complex.

* * *

Sean stopped and waited for the light to turn green. He glanced over at Tessa, unable to deny her complaint. He was relieved she'd be staying at home for this new tour of duty. He wanted her safe. Within six weeks, the fire season would come to a close. He wouldn't need to worry about her fighting fires anymore.

He gripped the steering wheel harder. The thought of never seeing her again twisted his heart. He'd been so angry, hurt and guilt-ridden when he'd broken off their engagement. But it had been the right thing to do. Hadn't it?

"I knew I shouldn't have worn my new boots this morning. I thought it'd be a good way to break them in before we went on a fire." Tessa huffed out a disgruntled sigh.

He chuckled, trying to ignore his morose thoughts. "You couldn't have known the new boots might cause you to sprain your ankle."

"Well, they did. I wish I'd worn something else today. You taught me better, but I didn't listen," she said.

He shook his head, thinking that her gutsy love of firefighting had been one of the reasons he'd been so drawn to her in the first place. "You'll be out of school soon, and then you won't have to think about such things. You'll move on to a desk job and start coordinating the crews that fight the fires."

She blinked. "You're right, of course. But I'll still be involved in all of it. Jared Marshall is an FMO and he still goes up on the fireline. You two men have taught me to be very hands on, no matter what my desk job might be. I think when the big boss is right there with the crews, they're able to do a better job."

Sean clenched his eyes closed for a moment. He should have known that Tessa would be the type of manager who wanted to be right in the middle of things instead of sitting safely in her office. He'd been trying so hard to watch over her, but he realized that was an impossible goal. He couldn't be with her twenty-four hours a day. He might protect her while they were on the fireline, but he couldn't keep her safe all the time. A car accident, illness, you name it. It was out of his hands. So what could he do? How could he keep her safe?

He couldn't, but God could. He needed to have faith. But honestly, he didn't know how to rely on the Lord. As a kid, he'd been on his own. He'd never trusted anyone, including God. And yet he sensed that putting his faith in his Heavenly Father was the only way he could ever find true happiness. If only he could let go of his fear.

"When you and Zach started fighting wildfires, it was only natural for me to sign up once I was old enough. I fell in love with fighting fires. It's a noble profession." She took a shuddering breath, staring out her window.

"After all that's happened, do you regret your career choice now?" he asked.

"No, not at all." She shook her head, speaking vehemently.

"That's a good thing with all the schooling you've acquired. You've worked hard for this. Is your ankle in much pain?" He wanted to change the topic.

"No, the pain pill they gave me has kicked in. I feel groggy," she said, breathing out a deep exhale and closing her eyes. No doubt she was feeling tranquil and sleepy.

"I'll get you home and then you can rest," he said.

He pulled into the parking lot of her apartment complex. Amidst her protests, he carried her up to her apartment, set her on the couch and helped her get comfortable. He retrieved a glass of water from the kitchen. When he leaned across her to place it close by on the coffee table, he felt her warmth and turned. Their noses touched. She looked deep into his eyes. Her breath tickled against his cheek. He felt lost and found all at the same time. Trapped in a gaze he couldn't escape. Transfixed.

He jerked away before he kissed her again. Before he said or did something else he might regret.

"It's time for me to go," he said.

"Yeah, the guys will be waiting for you." Her voice wobbled awkwardly.

But neither of them moved. Not for a very long time.

"Do you need anything else before I go?" he asked, stepping away.

"No. I'm just really tired now." She turned away and covered a yawn.

"I'll check in on you as soon as I get back in town. Try to take it easy."

He walked to the door, putting some distance between them, but it didn't help much. He paused, looking at her from over his shoulder. He hated to leave when she needed him, but maybe it was for the best.

She looked down at her hands clasped in her lap, her lips slightly parted. He knew she didn't like his silence, but she seemed so accepting. So patient.

"You be careful out there, okay?" she said, laying her head back.

It was his signal to leave. He nodded but didn't say a word. He couldn't trust his voice anymore.

He left as fast as he could. Before he changed his mind and scooped her into his arms. Before he spilled his guts, told her about his guilt then begged her forgiveness and asked her to take him back and never let him go. Because he knew she couldn't do that. Not if there was to be justice for Zach.

Chapter Fourteen

Three nights later the shrill ring of Tessa's cell phone brought her wide awake with a jerk. She fumbled around in the dark, trying to locate the phone on the nightstand beside her bed. She sat up and peered at the red glowing light of the clock radio. Two forty-eight in the morning. Who would be calling her at this hour? The hotshot crew was still fighting fire in Colorado.

Clutching the phone in her hand, she glanced at the caller ID and felt a flush of confusion. Cathy Morton. Why on earth would Matt's mother be calling her in the middle of the night?

Tessa punched the answer button. "Hello?"

Her voice sounded hoarse and groggy, but she was alert. Working on the hotshot crew, she was used to having her sleep interrupted. But not when it wasn't for a fire.

"Tessa?"

"Yes."

"This is Cathy Morton. I'm so very sorry to bother you at this time of night. Please forgive me, but is Sean there?"

Tessa blinked, wondering why the woman thought he'd be with her. They weren't married, after all. And they weren't really friends. They were just co-workers. "No, he's not."

"Oh, dear. I was hoping…" The woman's voice sounded sharp and distraught.

"What's up?" Tessa asked.

"It's Matt. He's at the police station. Apparently he went out with some of his old friends after I left for work tonight and they got pulled over for a DUI."

Oh, no. Tessa felt a sinking of disappointment.

"Was Matt drinking?" Tessa asked, her voice sounding normal now that she'd sat up and flung the covers off her legs.

She gently flexed her injured ankle and inwardly smiled when it didn't hurt too much. Three days of desk duty had almost done the trick, but she was lonely and bored. She missed her crew members, especially Sean. And she no longer fought it. In spite of her promise not to entangle her heart with him again, she missed him, worried about him and wanted him safe.

"No, Matt wasn't drinking, but the driver of the car was," Cathy said. "There were three other boys with him. One was Gavin Smith. Apparently he convinced Matt to go out with them tonight after I left for work. I've been worried about my son hanging around with that boy, but Matt won't listen. Now he's gotten himself into trouble again."

Gavin Smith. Tessa had been worried, too. It appeared that he'd pulled Matt back into his wild ways. And because she'd had so much optimism for both boys, this outcome made Tessa deeply sad.

"Because they were underage and out so late, the

police took all of the boys down to the station to wait for their parents," Cathy said.

"Is anyone hurt?"

"No, thankfully. The cops did a Breathalyzer test on all the boys, and Matt is the only one who passed. Otherwise, they said they would hold him until morning. But they want me to come down to the station to pick him up right now."

"At least no one was hurt. Matt can recover from this," Tessa said.

"Yes, but if he doesn't change his ways, he'll end up with a real problem on his hands." Cathy sounded near tears.

Tessa agreed. Gavin could be a good kid, if he chose to do so. But she didn't want him pulling Matt down with him if he was going to be getting into trouble.

"What do you need me to do?" Tessa asked.

"I'm at work. Other than the cook, I'm the only one on duty right now. I can't leave the diner. I would call Megan, but Jared left yesterday to go to a fire and she has two little kids at home who are undoubtedly sleeping at this hour. I don't want her to have to get them up. I tried to call Sean, but he's not picking up his phone. Matty told me he'd seen you over at his house the other day, so I thought maybe you and Sean were back together and he was with you. I was hoping he'd be willing to pick up Matt for me."

"No, Sean's not with me. He's on a fire in Colorado with the rest of the crew," Tessa said.

"Of course. I'll bet Jared is with them." The woman sounded deflated.

"I'll go get Matt," Tessa offered. She'd heard enough to know that Cathy was desperate. She couldn't refuse a cry for help. Not from a mother. And not when she knew how much Matt meant to Sean.

"Oh, would you? I'm deeply sorry for the bother, but I'd appreciate it so much," Cathy said. "I can call the police station and tell them you'll be coming to pick him up. They know I'm working tonight. If I ask them to, they shouldn't have a problem releasing Matt into your custody."

Thankfully, in a town this size, everyone knew almost everyone else. And it helped that Sean was good friends with Darrin Harper and a few of the other police officers. Darrin had been on the hotshot crew six years earlier, before he became a cop. Tessa hadn't worked with him, but he'd attended barbecues at her brother's apartment and she considered him a friend. She agreed that he should have no problem releasing Matt into her charge.

"All right, you call them and I'll get dressed," she said.

"Oh, thank you. I'll do that. And Tessa?"

"Yes?"

"You are a sweetheart, just like Sean said."

Tessa froze. Sean had said that about her? How odd.

"It's my pleasure to help," she said.

As she hung up the phone, she wondered about Sean. When he'd broken up with her, he'd said he didn't feel the same about her anymore. That they weren't right for each other and he didn't want to marry her. But now that she thought about it, not once had he told her that he didn't love her anymore. So maybe he still loved her. She was almost positive of it. It was in his touch, and his kiss. She'd known Sean for a long time. He needed help. He needed her. She'd tried everything she could think of to get him to open up and let her in. She'd be leaving town soon to return to school, but there was nothing else she could do. Except pray and hope that God could soften Sean's heart.

Within minutes Tessa arrived at the police station. It wasn't very big. A small red-brick building set up on an empty lot owned by the city on the outskirts of town.

She pulled into a parking space beside a squad car and shut off the headlights to her truck. Killing the engine, she climbed out. The crisp night air embraced her and she shivered. She reached for her jacket. As she slid her arms into the sleeves, she looked up. Two tall streetlights gleamed overhead as she made her way up the front sidewalk. Crickets chirped in the bushes edging the small plot of lawn. She pushed against the double doors and stepped inside the main foyer. The heavy aroma of coffee struck her in the face.

"Hi, there, Tessa."

Darrin Harper sat behind the reception counter, leaning back in his chair. Wearing his police uniform, he reached his hands high over his head and stretched. He appeared to be the only officer on duty. Not surprising in a town this size. They only had three officers, not to mention the late hour. Sandy Coolidge, their dispatcher, was probably home sleeping soundly.

Tessa's gaze lowered to the gun holstered at his hip. "Hello, Darrin. I understand you have Matt Morton in here."

He smiled. "Yep. Cathy just called to say you'd be picking him up and taking him home. That's nice of you."

She nodded, feeling out of sorts. She wished Sean

was here and realized how much she depended on him in difficult situations like this. He always knew what to do and what was right.

"If you'll wait right here, I'll go get Matt," Darrin said.

"Is Gavin Smith still here, as well?"

"Yeah, he'll be here overnight…until his grandpa can pick him up in the morning."

"Can I see him?" She didn't know what made her ask. She only knew that she hated to lose him as much as she hated losing Matt. If she saw Gavin, she wasn't sure what she'd say to him, but she didn't want to just write him off as a lost cause. Everyone was important. Even the Savior left the ninety-and-nine sheep to find the one lost lamb. Maybe Gavin just needed to know that someone cared about him.

Darrin hiked one eyebrow and stood. "Nope, sorry. No visitors for him tonight."

The disappointment must have shown on her face because he rested a hand on her shoulder.

"Trust me, Tessa. You don't want to see him right now. He's falling down drunk and mean and foul-mouthed. He needs to sleep it off. Maybe you can visit him later, after he gets out of jail."

Her heart gave a painful thump. She hated the thought that this teenage boy was inebriated. Maybe Sean would have some ideas on what to do. But ultimately, Gavin would have to decide to help himself.

"I'll go get Matt," Darrin said.

She leaned against the front counter as the officer walked through a door to the back rooms. Clutching her car keys in one hand, she waited. Looking around, she glanced at a bulletin board that included mug shots of the FBI's most wanted and various other public notices.

"Tessa!"

She whirled around and faced Matt. He stood in the doorway wearing faded blue jeans and a T-shirt. His thick brown hair was disheveled, his face pale, his eyes wide with contrition.

"Hi, Matt. You ready to go home?" she asked.

"Where...where's my mom?" He blinked in confusion.

"She called me from her work and asked if I'd come and get you. I told her I'd bring you home."

His eyes lowered to the floor and he scuffed the toe of his tennis shoe against the gray carpet. "Oh. I'm sorry. She had to wake you up, didn't she?"

She patted his arm. "It's okay, sweetie. I'm available for you anytime, day or night. So are Sean and your mom. We've got your back. One of us will always be here for you."

"Yeah, I'm sorry I caused trouble for her. Where is Sean?" he asked.

She explained about the wildfire and he let out a breath of relief. "So he's not here in town right now?"

"No."

"Good. I don't want him to see me in this place." He tossed a sheepish frown toward Darrin.

Without asking, she understood his reasons. "Let's get you out of here, then."

"Just one more thing," Darrin said to Tessa. He slid several papers onto the counter and pointed at two lines. "Sign here and here."

She did so then turned to go.

"Stay out of trouble," Darrin called to the boy with a serious look.

Matt flushed red as a new fire engine and nodded, not meeting the officer's eyes.

Outside, Matt didn't speak much as Tessa drove him to his mobile home on Fourth Street.

"Your mom said to take you home. Are you sure you'll be okay alone?" she asked.

"Yeah, I just want to go to sleep now. I'm really sorry you had to come and get me like this," he said.

"I know." She gripped the steering wheel as she drove down the dark, abandoned streets.

"You…you won't tell Sean about it, will you? I promised him I'd behave myself, and I… I've let him down again."

The kid looked so forlorn, so miserable, that Tessa figured his guilty conscience was eating him up inside. And she couldn't help wondering if it was the same for Sean. Was his conscience eating him up, too?

"No, I won't tell Sean," Tessa said. "It's enough that your mom knows about it. But you're old enough to understand that she has her hands full earning a living for you. You're not helping to ease her load by getting into trouble. She wanted to be here but couldn't abandon her responsibilities at work. She needs her job so she can provide for you, to pay the bills and put food in your mouth. You've left her in a difficult position."

He stared at the floor, looking completely ashamed. "I know. I'm sorry. I never meant to hurt her. I'll do better from now on. I promise."

"You should tell her that," Tessa said. "What made you decide to get into the car with those boys anyway?"

She didn't look at him as she asked the question. She

couldn't help thinking that everyone deserved a second chance. Including her and Sean.

Matt shrugged. "Gavin said we were just going for a ride. We were dragging Main Street, you know? Just hanging out with my friends."

"Hmm, they don't sound like friends to me. Not if they'd do things to get you into trouble," Tessa said.

Matt lowered his head. "Yeah, I guess not. Everything was fine until Gavin pulled out a bottle of whiskey. I didn't have any, though. I told Sean I wouldn't drink anymore, and I kept my word. But I was already in the car and couldn't get out. I asked them to take me home, but they wouldn't. And Gavin got mad at me. Before I knew what was happening, a cop pulled us over. I didn't have a choice."

"Yes, you did," she said. "You knew what those boys were like. You made a choice the moment you got into the car with them, Matt. Now you've got to make it right. Steer clear of them. They're no good for you."

He nodded, looking humble and repentant. "I know. I won't be hanging out with Gavin anymore, I can tell you that. And I tried to do what was right by not drinking. At least I did that right."

"Yes, you did that right. But I suggest you pick some new friends, like those in your Boy Scout group."

He peeked at her in a hesitant glance that showed his fear. "Do you think Sean will find out?"

Funny how he was so desperate for Sean to not find out what he had done. Sean would forgive him, of course. Matt had been foolish to get in the car with the boys, but it wasn't his fault they'd started drinking. He'd simply allowed himself to get sucked into a bad situation. It was undoubtedly the same for Sean. When

Zach had died, he'd found himself in an impossible position. One that almost got him killed, too. But now it was time for him to heal.

"You promise you won't tell him?" Matt pressed.

"I promise. But I think you should keep your word to Sean, too. Especially since you know it's for your own good. No more hanging out with a bad crowd."

Matt inclined his head. She caught a glimpse of Sean in his eyes. How much he wanted to be accepted. How badly he needed someone he could trust. Someone to depend upon. And that made people do crazy things sometimes. But this boy still needed a friend right now. And Sean did, too. When he'd broken off their engagement, she'd been devastated and felt like he was abandoning her. It had made her suspect that he had done something to get Zach killed. But maybe when he'd pushed her away, his actions had really been a cry for help. And when she'd left town, she had been the one who had abandoned him when he needed her the most.

"You're right," Matt agreed.

"The other boys might blab. It's a small town and you know how gossip travels quickly. Sean could still find out from someone else," she warned.

Horror ignited in Matt's eyes. His face drained of all color, looking pale in the dim light. He covered his eyes with his hands. "Oh, no."

"It's not the end of the world. You can start fresh right now. I think you'll find that Sean can be quite forgiving," she said.

Another nod as he threaded his fingers together and clenched them tight. "If Sean finds out, he might not want to be friends with me anymore."

"That's not true. Sean loves you. He'd never abandon you." Tessa knew what she said was true. And that was when she realized how much this boy craved a father figure. Someone he could believe in. Someone to love him unconditionally. It gave her insight into Sean's mind-set, too. He'd been raised in foster care. He probably didn't believe he could depend on her support. No wonder he'd pushed her away when Zach had died. And she had let him. She'd put her own pain first. She'd been hurting so badly that she couldn't see what was really going on. The survivor's guilt. The pain of losing his best friend.

She parked in Matt's driveway and killed the engine. Looking at the small trailer house where he lived with his mother, she thought Matt could do much worse. At least he had a place to belong. A home and a mom who loved him. Likewise, Tessa still had her mother. But Sean had no one. Not anymore.

"I don't think Sean's friendship is so shallow that he'd abandon you just because you were in a car with boys who were drinking," she said. "But friends shouldn't keep secrets from each other. When the time's right, you ought to tell Sean what you did and that you're sorry."

He met her eyes. "I will. And thanks for coming to get me, Tessa."

She smiled. "You're welcome."

A week later the hotshot crew returned to town. The following day they cleaned out their gear and restocked their fuel supplies. Tessa was so happy to have them back that she set up a long table outside near the garage. She spread a cheap, plastic covering over the tabletop then laid out two platters of sandwiches, chips, cookies and cold drinks for the men to enjoy. A welcome-home celebration.

The men ate and talked as they repaired their equipment. Ace eyed Tessa's ankle as she walked past him. "Don't tell me you faked that sprain just so you could get out of going on that fire with us."

She laughed, surprised that she didn't feel irritated by his teasing. "Yeah, sure I did. You've got me pegged, Ace."

The men chuckled and she enjoyed the lighthearted banter around her. She'd had over a week for her ankle to heal and it felt almost as good as new. Now she was ready to get back to work. But a cloud hung over her. She wanted to have a talk with Sean and wondered how to broach the topic on her mind. She couldn't explain it, but she felt better when he was near. They hadn't resolved the barriers between them, but that didn't seem to matter anymore.

As she worked outside in the yard to maintain their transport buggies, Sean's gaze rested on her. Her senses went on high alert. He'd come home with a week's worth of stubble on his face, but he'd shaven it off first thing. Standing nearby, he wore a clean hotshot uniform, his dark hair glimmering in the afternoon sunshine.

"Are you really doing okay?" he asked.

"Of course. I'm fine," she said.

"Good. I'm glad you got some rest while we were gone. But we missed you." He sounded sincere.

His words touched her heart. He'd been protecting her so much that she'd begun to doubt her place on the crew. His words reassured her.

He turned and walked toward the garage, leaving the

air filled with an aching loneliness. He paused beside a stack of shovels and started counting them.

"Yeah, I can see the two of you don't like each other at all." Ace blurted the words, winning a dark glàre from Sean.

"Get back to work," Sean called.

"Sure thing, super." With a good-natured shrug, Ace picked up a pile of Pulaskis and carried them into the tool shop for sharpening.

"Thanks for the grub," Harlie called to Tessa as he snatched up another sandwich.

"Yeah, thanks, Tess." The other men smiled their gratitude, munching on a huge bowl of potato chips.

"You're welcome."

The crunch of gravel caused her to turn. A police car pulled into the yard. Darrin Harper got out and walked toward them, a lazy grin on his face. He was dressed in his police uniform, with a silver badge pinned to his chest that gleamed in the sunlight.

Tessa's heart sank. Oh, no. This couldn't be good. What was the cop doing here in the middle of the afternoon?

"Darrin! How you doing, buddy?" Sean greeted the man with a wave of his hand.

"Hi, Sean. I'm good." The officer rested his fingers lightly against the black gun on his hip.

"Are you hungry? Help yourself," Tessa offered, hoping to sidetrack him long enough to ask him to keep quiet about Matt.

The deputy accepted a cold soft drink but declined the food. If only Sean would move away long enough for her to speak with Darrin for a moment. But he didn't budge.

"Looks like you're busy today," Darrin said.

"Yeah, we just got back from a fire yesterday. What brings you out to our neighborhood?" Sean asked.

Tessa dipped a large sponge into a bucket of soapy water before slathering it onto the fender of one of the crew's transport buggies. As she washed the vehicle, she half listened to the conversation.

"I just wanted to stop by and check up on how Matt Morton is doing," Darrin said.

Tessa froze. Since Sean had returned yesterday, she had no idea if Matt had seen him and told him about his trip to the police station. The officer undoubtedly knew about Sean's work with Matt, but she felt a fissure of loyalty to the boy. She didn't want Darrin to spill the beans. Not until Matt was ready for Sean to know the truth.

And that thought stopped her in her tracks. Was that what Sean was doing? Waiting until he was ready to talk about Zach's death? That didn't make sense. And yet it did. But what if Sean was never ready to talk about it? He might keep it bottled up inside himself forever. And she was no longer willing to leave it up to chance.

"I think Matt is doing well," Sean said.

"No more riding around in cars with drunk drivers, right?" Darrin asked.

Sean tilted his head to one side, his brows curved in a quizzical frown. Oh, boy. Here it was. What if Sean didn't know?

"Hey, Darrin," she called, trying to distract the two men.

The man turned toward her. "Yes?"

"How's your family doing?" she asked.

"They're all good," he said.

"Do you—" she began, but Sean cut her off.

"What do you mean, drunk drivers?" he asked, his voice elevated slightly.

Darrin shifted his weight and focused back on Sean. He took a sip of his soft drink. "Didn't Matt tell you?"

Sean shook his head. "Tell me what?"

Tessa braced herself, choking the damp sponge with her hands. In a few short sentences, Darrin filled Sean in on what had happened last week.

"I just saw him last night and he didn't say a word," Sean said.

"Cathy was working late at the diner, so she called Tessa to pick Matt up at the police station. Apparently you were out of town on a wildfire," Darrin said.

Sean's gaze shifted over to Tessa, his eyes boring a hole in her head like a high-speed drill. A dark premonition washed over her and she wished Darrin would shut his big mouth. She would rather Matt was the first person to tell Sean what had happened. No matter what, the jig was up. Sean knew everything now.

She had to give Sean some credit. He played it cool. He didn't overreact. He didn't say another word about it. The two men talked a few minutes more. Then Darrin got into his squad car and pulled out of the yard. Even though this wasn't the cop's fault, Tessa was glad to see him go.

"Why didn't you tell me?"

She snapped her head up and found Sean standing directly behind her. "Tell you what?"

The corners of his mouth tipped up in a tight look of exasperation. "That Matt had been pulled into the police station because he was in a car where the other boys were drinking alcohol and he called you to pick him up."

"It was Cathy who called me to pick him up. And Matt wasn't driving the car. He hadn't been drinking, Sean."

"Exactly. Why didn't you tell me all of that?"

She shrugged. "It wasn't my place. Matt made me promise not to. Besides, Cathy knows all about it. She's his mom. He was embarrassed and regretted it, but he was planning to tell you when he was ready."

Sean's eyes filled with accusation. "Matt is a sixteen-year-old boy. You should have told me, Tess. I have a right to know."

She shook her head. "No, you don't. Cathy called my place in the middle of the night, looking for you. You weren't in town, so I helped out. That's all. But that didn't obligate me to tell you about it. Especially since Matt made me promise to be quiet about it."

"Why would he do that?"

She dropped the sponge into the bucket of water and wiped her wet hands on her pants. "Oh, let me think. Maybe because he really likes you and doesn't want to let you down again. He's afraid you won't like him anymore. That you won't still be his friend. He doesn't want to hurt you."

"That's silly. I'll always be his friend," he said.

"Of course you will, and I told him so. He made a mistake by getting in the car with those boys, but the drinking wasn't his fault. I hope you won't make it worse by making a big issue out of it. You have to forgive him. That's what you do when you love someone," she said.

Sean froze. For a flickering moment his eyes flashed with despair. And that was when Tessa realized what she'd said. How unfair she sounded. How hypocritical she'd been. No, he hadn't abandoned her. Not really. She'd walked away from him. When he'd broken off their engagement, she'd left town without another word to him. And now she regretted it. No matter how hard he tried to push her away, she should have stayed by his side and silently supported him until he was ready to talk to her.

"I've been worried about that boy, Tessa. You know I've been watching out for him and Gavin, too," Sean said.

"I know. But I made a promise and I couldn't break it. I was just trying to protect Matt," she said.

The same way Sean was always trying to protect her. She understood that now.

"Matt still needs lots of guidance. You should have talked to me about it," he said.

Frustration boiled up inside her. "Maybe you're right. Maybe I should have told you, just like you should have talked to me about Zach."

His face darkened in a thunderous expression. Something cold and hard filled his eyes. Without a word, he turned and walked to the office building. She didn't follow after him as he disappeared into the shadows of tall elm trees lining the front sidewalk. She figured he needed time alone. They both did. But she stood there, mute and shaking, and stared at the sparkling clean truck she'd been scrubbing. Unable to work. Unable to move. Unable to think clearly. She only hoped she hadn't finally pushed Sean over the edge.

Sean walked straight into his office. He pulled a key from his pants pocket, opened the right hand drawer to his desk and jerked out a large, sealed manila envelope.

It contained a notebook filled with his shaky handwriting. His personal notes on what had happened the day that Zach had died. Whenever any of them faced a traumatic experience, the psychiatrist always encouraged them to write down their thoughts and feelings as part of the therapy of healing. Tessa and the other crew members all knew about this exercise and usually laughed about it. But Sean didn't feel like laughing now. He held the notebook in his hands, his entire body quaking. He thought about what he was planning to do and wondered if it was another big mistake.

His silence had created more suspicion. It had driven a wedge between him and Tessa. But now he had to let it go. She had a right to know what had happened. He just hoped she wouldn't hate him afterward.

Slamming the desk drawer, he walked back outside and straight toward Tessa. She stood where he'd left her, drying off one of the vehicles with a soft cloth from the rag box. Most of the men were inside, giving them a bit of privacy.

As Sean approached, Tessa's mouth dropped open and she met his gaze. He caught a glimmer of confusion in her eyes.

He spoke low, for her ears alone. "I've made a mistake, Tessa. I was trying to keep you safe, just like you were doing for Matt. I realize now that I was wrong to do so. I hope reading these notes will make you happy and finally bring you some peace. But I doubt it."

He slapped the envelope down on the hood of the truck then turned and walked back to the office.

His throat felt tight, his lungs burning. A powerful doubt overshadowed him but he kept moving. His heart pounded inside his chest. He couldn't turn back the hands of time and undo all the bad that had happened. He couldn't change the outcome, no matter how much he wished he could. But over the past weeks, he and Tessa had worked with each other. They'd learned how to get along and even shared some fun and laughter. It had given Sean the hope that they might be friends again. That maybe they could be more than friends. But as soon as she read his notes, he feared that would die. She might never be able to forgive him. But if he ever hoped to recover from his PTSD and win her back, he had to take the chance. He had to let her know everything. Because no matter what, he would never stop loving her.

Chapter Fifteen

At one fifteen the following morning the shrill ring of Sean's cell phone awoke him from a dead sleep. Dispatch calling to tell him that they had a desert fire burning in the hills south of Reno. Their home turf.

Sitting up in bed, Sean turned on the bedside lamp. He made several calls, waking his squad bosses first. He knew they'd contact each crew member serving under them. Within an hour they'd all congregate at the hotshot base where they'd load up and depart within a matter of minutes. They were ready, their saws and tools cleaned, their fuel containers filled.

Sean thought about calling Tessa himself but decided he should work through the hierarchy of the team. He wondered if her ankle was healed enough for the heavy work on a fireline, but she already felt singled out by him. No need to make it any worse.

By five in the morning the crew was loaded up and tailing a line of pumper trucks along a narrow desert road that shot across gullies and low-lying ridges. The desert spread out for miles around them, covered with brittle sagebrush and clumps of dried cheatgrass. The golden glow of dawn greeted them from the east as the crew transport came to a jarring stop.

"Everyone out," Sean called as they arrived at their destination.

A few moans and wide yawns greeted him as the men sat up and peered with bleary eyes out the windows.

"That was a fast ride. Not much time to nap," Dean grumbled.

Looking toward the back of the buggie, Sean saw Tessa watching him, her tired eyes filled with an emotion he couldn't discern. He wondered if she'd read his notes and figured she must have. The empty space between them seemed to fill up with all the words he'd left unsaid.

She grabbed her Pulaski, the only person fully awake and ready to vacate the vehicle. He waited patiently while the men lined past him and unloaded. Mumbled groans were the only sounds to fill the dry, hot August air.

The fire was burning sideways across the low-lying hills a couple of miles southeast of them. Great clouds of smoke billowed up from the crown of a rocky, grass-covered mound. Trying to focus on his work, Sean remembered his goal and gave instructions.

"Line out and hold the fire's advance right here." He gestured to the area where they should work.

The crew tooled up and lined out in quick unison, approaching the fire from the west. With no trees to cut down, the sawyers left their chain saws back in the buggies. Each crew member carried hand tools instead.

The team worked for some time in numbing monotony. Gusts of wind buffeted them, intensifying the sweaty heat. A squawk from his radio pulled Sean away from his task.

He depressed the call button. "Go ahead."

"We've got a civilian who is refusing to leave his cabin," the dispatcher said.

"Well, what do you want me to do about it?" Sean returned.

"Get him outta there," came the brusque reply.

Sean heaved a weary sigh. The crew didn't need this right now, but he obediently pressed the button one more time. "Will do."

He got the coordinates then waved to get Harlie's attention.

The squad leader jogged over to him, puffing breath. "What's up, super?"

"Bring one more crew member and come with me. We've got a little errand to run."

Shaking his head, Sean peered at the dirt road, searching through the floating smoke for some sign of the cabin. He saw it, sitting among a scattered grove of pinion-junipers, called PJ's for short.

Without looking back, he started forward, jogging along the dirt road at a fast clip. When he turned he saw Harlie and Tessa running beside him and froze. No, not Tessa. What was Harlie thinking?

He tossed an irritated glance at the squad leader, but Harlie wasn't looking at him and never noticed. But Tessa did.

With a slight lift of her chin, she gazed at Sean without blinking, her bloodshot eyes almost daring him to send her away. She undoubtedly knew he wanted to ask for someone else. To leave her behind. But he couldn't. Not now. There wasn't time.

Resigned to the situation, he lifted a hand. "Follow me."

He rushed down the path. The fire was moving toward them fast, but they had the expanse of desert and road to shelter them. For the time being. A burst of urgency swept over him. If they didn't want to get caught in the flames, they'd have to hurry.

"What are we doing here, super?" Harlie yelled the words over the rapidly increasing drone of the fire.

"We're gonna bring out a civilian before he and his cabin get burned to cinders," Sean said.

"Why didn't he evacuate with the other home owners?" Harlie asked.

Sean shrugged.

"If the fool wants to burn, then I say let him go," Harlie said.

Sean agreed, but he didn't say so. He was angry that someone was endangering all of their lives for a stupid house that could be replaced. But they kept running forward, following orders. Putting their lives on the line to save someone who could have left earlier and been safe now.

A few more minutes and they saw the man. He stood outside his cabin, using a skimpy garden hose to spray the flickering flames that licked at the dried timbers.

Sean hurried up to him and tapped him on the shoulder. The man jerked around. "Oh, you startled me."

"What's your name?" Sean asked.

"Dwight Connor, and I'm sure glad to see you. Help me put out this fire, will you? I can't lose my cabin."

Gazing at the inferno boiling around them, Sean snorted. Defending this cabin was like trying to hold back the tides of the ocean. It was futile and ridiculous and would only cost their lives.

"No, sir. You need to come with us right now. Your cabin is lost. If you stay here, you will most certainly die," Sean said.

The balding man barely spared the firefighters a glance, his face, cotton shirt and blue jeans covered with soot. "No, I won't go. I'm staying right here. I can hold the fire off. I don't want to lose my vacation home."

Vacation home? That was all the man was thinking about? He just didn't get it. This wasn't about him anymore. He was risking many people's lives now.

Sean glanced at Harlie and Tessa. They shifted nervously, their eyes filled with fear and urgency. He wished he'd come alone. They knew what he knew. That this was a losing proposition. If anything happened to Tessa, he didn't think he could bear the pain. He wouldn't be able to live with himself. If they didn't want to die today, their only chance was to get out of here. Right. Now.

"That piddly hose isn't going to do one bit of good against this fire. We're leaving. Now," Sean yelled above the roar of the quickly advancing flames.

"Then so be it," Dwight yelled back.

No way. Sean knew even if Dwight stayed here of his own accord that his family would hold the hotshot crew accountable for his death. Sean could almost see the headlines now. Minoa Hotshot Crew abandons poor, defenseless home owner to flames.

The stupid wretch.

Whipping out his sharp lock-blade knife, Sean walked over to the tap and slit the hose in two. He picked it up and carried it over to Dwight where he dropped it at the man's feet.

"Try putting the fire out with that," Sean said.

"Hey! What'd you do that for?" Dwight blustered.

"You have two options. Walk out with us right now, or get carried out unconscious," Sean said.

When he looked at Harlie, Dwight's eyes widened. The firefighter's gaze was filled with raw anger and he held his Pulaski like a club as if he'd like to hit Dwight over the head with it.

Just to their right, a cluster of PJ's exploded into flame. They all jerked and ducked their heads. The heat felt like a furnace against their flesh.

"Okay, okay. I'll go," Dwight said, holding his hands up in surrender.

"This way!" Tessa pointed to an opening among the PJ's.

"No! Head for the road," Sean yelled.

She hesitated, her eyes filled with doubt and fear. "But it's filled with smoke. And where there's smoke, there's fire. We can't go that way."

He clasped her arm, gazing into her eyes for just a moment. "I know what I'm doing, Tessa. Trust me. Please."

She tilted her head, her eyes wide with disbelief. For several pounding moments he thought she might refuse and go the other way. Just like Zach. And heaven help him, if she ran into the trees, Sean would follow her... and die with her. He would not leave her no matter what. No turning away. Never again. Not for him.

She nodded and turned toward the road. And her vote of confidence meant everything to him. It gave him the courage to lead them forward.

As a group, they sprinted for their lives. An urgent flush of adrenaline pushed Sean onward. He didn't have time to be scared. All he could think about at that moment was getting Tessa out of there. Keeping her safe. Throughout the fire season, he'd tried so hard to save her life, and now she might lose it in spite of his best efforts.

A fifteen-foot wall of fire paralleled the dirt road, rising and arching over their heads. Like a sea of flame, it rolled and churned, headed straight for them. The intense heat burned them through their Nomex shirts. Sean knew it would be even worse for Dwight, who wore no fire-resistant clothing. The roar of a freight train filled his ears, crashing down on top of them.

As they raced down the dirt road, Sean could barely see through to the end of the tunnel. And that was when he prayed. For the first time since Zach had died. Asking God's forgiveness for giving up on Him. Asking for His help. Promising anything if the Lord would just get them out of here safely. Because he loved Tessa. He always had. He always would. There was no use denying it any longer.

If they hurried, they might make it out alive. If they failed, they'd be hailed on the national news as heroes who had tried to save Dwight Connor's life. And Sean didn't want to be a hero today.

White-hot panic forced Tessa to hurry faster. She pumped her legs hard, her lungs burning for oxygen. She'd heard it said once that every man turned to prayer when he was in the midst of battle, and she supposed that was true. And as she felt the blaze intensify, felt its scorching heat against her face, she prayed like never before. Asking God to shelter them. Asking Him to get them out safely.

Like always, Sean shepherded them from behind.

Harlie ran beside her, with Dwight Connor in back. She could hear Sean's hoarse voice directly over her right shoulder, but the thundering blare of the fire drowned out his words. It didn't matter. She understood him well enough. Run! Get out of here now.

Looking ahead, she saw an opening not thirty feet away. If they could make it, they'd be safe.

Dwight stumbled and fell, his hand grazing her arm as he slammed into the dirt. Her stride slowed and she hesitated. Sean stopped to help the man up. No, no! They didn't have time.

She whirled around, turning back for Sean. But Harlie grabbed her web belt and jerked her forward.

"Come on! Sean's got him," Harlie yelled.

Glancing over her shoulder, she saw that Sean had Dwight back on his feet. The civilian was limping. Sean wrapped his arm around the man's waist and pushed him onward.

"Go! Go!" Sean's voice sounded small and insignificant amidst the fire, clogged by fear or soot. She wasn't sure which. Maybe both.

Thinking he was right behind her, Tessa kept going. Five more paces and she darted into safety. Her crew members dragged her and Harlie away from the wall of flames. She lifted her head and saw the shadowy specter of several huge pumper trucks, their large hoses dousing the blaze with a deluge of water. Those trucks were the only things holding back the encroaching firestorm. A thin line that separated the hotshot crew from certain death. The team was moving away from the intense heat, but they were short a man.

Sean!

She looked back, seeking him within the smoke. Where was he? Why wasn't he here with her?

The flames closed off sight to him and Dwight, engulfing them in a churning melee of orange and yellow fire. She coughed, a thick hacking sound.

Where was Sean? Where was he?

"Sean! Sean!" she screamed over and over again.

She darted toward the flames, desperate to save him. Desperate to tell him that she hadn't read his personal notes. That it didn't matter to her anymore. Nothing mattered now, except for being with him.

Her heart felt as though it would burst within her chest. She couldn't lose him now. Not like this. She loved him still. She knew that now. She'd been hurt and angry, wanting answers. But it hadn't killed her love. And she wanted one last chance to tell him so. She didn't want to live without him in her life. She had to reach him. She must!

Harlie pulled her back. "No, Tessa. You can't help him now."

"I can. I can," she insisted, fighting Harlie's hold.

Dean and Ace raced to stop her. She clawed at them as they hugged her tight. Held immobile by her crew members, she sobbed her anguish, filled with utter despair.

She'd lost Zach. Her dear, sweet brother was gone. And now she would lose Sean, too. The love of her life.

The sky above was surrounded by thick, black smoke. The sun was a round, blood-red haze that seemed to taunt them. She felt helpless. Lost and hopeless.

Alone.

A shiver swept her in spite of the tremendous heat. A wall of flame engulfed the area where Sean had been limping along with Dwight. The roar of the fire filled her ears, deafening her. All she heard was the pounding of her heart.

Sean was gone. She'd lost him for good this time.

The erratic winds pushed the flames apart, squeezing a small alcove along the dirt road. Like the Red Sea, the fire parted. In the swirling heat, two images emerged at the tiny opening.

"Sean!" she yelled.

He was dragging Dwight in the dirt. Crouched low, he trudged on, his shoulders hunched as he pulled the limp figure to safety.

The hotshot crew ran to help. Harlie and Dean released Tessa and she hurried to Sean's side. Like walking through a curtain, he emerged from the flames and collapsed in her arms. She sat on the ground, bending over him. He smiled up at her, his eyes bloodshot, his white teeth flashing in a face blackened by smoke and blisters.

"I got him out. I didn't leave him behind. I got him out safe," Sean's voice croaked. And then he closed his eyes and went limp.

Chapter Sixteen

Sean sat in the maintenance shop alone, his eyes gritty with fatigue. Days had passed since the fire when he'd pulled Dwight Connor out of the flames. Even with the pain pills Sean had been given in the hospital for the burns he'd received, he hadn't been sleeping well. In time, his physical wounds would heal, but not the wounds in his heart.

Tessa had sat beside his bed in the hospital, holding his bandaged hand, but they didn't speak much. When he'd gotten out, he'd thought about calling or driving over to her apartment, but changed his mind a dozen times. They had to talk, but he dreaded it. He didn't want to hurt her anymore. She deserved to be happy.

Careful of his blistered hands, he moved the blade of his pocket knife in a circular motion over a flat, rectangular sharpening stone. At ten minutes after seven Tessa walked inside, before the rest of the crew arrived for work. He looked up, feeling her presence before he saw her. Funny how connected he felt to this woman he'd tried so hard to push away.

Her quiet gaze rested on him like a thunderous shout. She gripped a manila envelope in one hand. His notebook.

Here it was. The moment he'd been dreading. It was inevitable. Like the sea rushing to the shore. But now his reprieve had ended.

Without a word, she walked over and set the envelope on the workbench. His gaze rested on it.

"It's still sealed," he said.

"Yes. I didn't read it."

"Why not?"

"It doesn't matter to me. I don't care what's in your notes, nor do I care what happened in the past. I only care about you."

He blinked at her, trying to absorb her words, wondering what to say. But he had to talk. Had to tell her everything. If he was ever to heal from his PTSD and have a second chance with her, then he couldn't keep any secrets from her. Not ever.

She leaned her hip against the workbench and silently waited for him to speak. Her eyes questioned him, her shoulders tense. It was time.

Taking a deep breath, he sat back on his tall stool and clenched his eyes closed. Nothing could prepare him for this. It didn't help that Jared Marshall had visited him in the hospital the day before to inform him that he was going to receive a special commendation, along with Harlie and Tessa, for saving Dwight Connor's life.

Sean had snorted at the news. He didn't deserve it for two reasons. First, he'd still like to throttle Connor's neck for almost getting them all killed. And second, because he still felt responsible for Zach's death. And yet the guilt no longer seemed so oppressive.

"You know Zach and I were trying to get a jump on

the fire." His voice sounded hoarse from the smoke and heat he'd inhaled a few days earlier.

"Yes, I know. But you don't need to explain it to me, Sean. Truly, it doesn't matter anymore." Tessa spoke so softly that he almost didn't hear her.

He let the memories wash over him in painful waves. "But I do need to explain. I need to tell you so I can finally let it go."

She didn't say anything and he began again. "Zach wouldn't follow me. He ran toward a creek bed instead."

"Gosser's Creek," she said.

"Yes, the same creek where Jared and Megan and their kids had taken refuge. Except that they were located farther down, where the creek widened out and the water provided a lot more security for them. But the position where Zach and I were located offered nothing but a narrow trickle of water. Even if we could make it there in time, I knew there was no way we could survive the burnover."

He heard her swallow, but she waited for him to continue.

"When I tried to stop him, he slugged me in the face and knocked me down. When I got back up, I couldn't see him through the smoke. I yelled and yelled for him to come back. I had no idea where he'd gone until hours later, when they found his body." Sean opened his eyes, the memories drenching him like sheets of icy rain.

"He panicked," Tessa said, her voice sounding small and uncertain as though she couldn't believe it.

Sean nodded without looking at her, licking his cracked lips. "Yes, and I couldn't stop him, Tessa. I tried. Oh, how I tried. But I had only moments to make a choice. I could hurry into the previously burned area and deploy my own shelter, or chase after Zach and die with him. I couldn't do both." He paused, his voice wavering. "I chose life. All I could think about was getting back to you. Loving you. Being with you always. But now I wonder if it was selfish of me to do so. I wanted to live. More than anything else on earth. I lay there in my fire shelter and listened to Zach's screams and I couldn't do a single thing to save him."

A horrible, swelling silence followed. Moisture clogged his eyes. Tears ran down her cheeks, too. He hated that he had made her cry again. Hated for her to know that her brother died a long, painful death.

"It wasn't your fault, Sean," she finally said. "When they recovered Zach's body, they discovered he was missing his gloves. But you were so secretive and refused to talk to me so I thought perhaps you'd done something else to cause his death. Now, I realize that isn't so."

"Yes, Zach lost his gloves and it was my fault," he confirmed.

She stared at him and her eyes widened. "No, it wasn't."

He looked down. "Yes it was. Gloves can make the difference between life and death. Without them, Zach couldn't hold on to his fire shelter during the intense heat. I remember during an earlier rest period that day, he'd laid his gloves down while we ate our lunch. When we moved on, he must have forgotten to pick them up again."

"But that wasn't your error," she reiterated, her voice choked by tears.

A fresh bout of emotion slammed into him and he gulped a shaky breath. "I should have given him mine.

If I'd been paying attention, I would have noticed he'd lost his gloves. He was working under me. He was my concern. I should have made certain that he was okay, even if it meant giving him my gloves."

"No," she cried. "Every hotshot knows they need their gloves to do their work. It's a standard piece of equipment. It was Zach's responsibility. No one expected you to forfeit your own life for him."

"But he was my friend. The Savior said that there is no greater love than to lay down your life for your friends. I should have done that for Zach. If I'd been more vigilant, I could have ensured he had gloves. I could have made him come with me."

She shook her head. "How? He fought you, Sean. Even with gloves, Zach might still have died. He panicked and ran the wrong way. The fire was too intense for him to survive even if he could have held on to his fire shelter. You couldn't force him to go with you. Not without dying, too. And that wouldn't have been right. I don't believe God would want you to throw away your own life like that. I wouldn't want it, either."

He lifted his gaze, his heart in his throat. "Do you really mean that?"

"Yes! I absolutely do."

He couldn't deny the conviction in her voice, or on her face. He knew she was speaking the truth. And her trust in him meant so much. It meant everything.

"I've learned that I need to have more faith," he said. "That I need to trust in the Lord. I need to trust in you, too. I didn't think that you could ever forgive me after what happened to Zach. That you would blame me. I'm sorry I couldn't save him, Tessa. So very sorry."

She made a small noise as if she was trying to contain her emotion. Then she flung her arms around his neck, holding tight. He flinched, his body still sore from the various superficial burns he'd received during their most recent fire. He couldn't fight her anymore. Not now. Not when she knew everything. Not when he loved her so much.

"It wasn't your fault, Sean. I'm telling you, it wasn't your fault. And you know I wouldn't say it if it wasn't true. So you've got to believe me. I love you. I always will. There's nothing you can say or do to make me stop."

Her words rushed over him like a cleansing balm. Soothing his pain. Bringing the comfort he'd craved for so long.

"The Atonement of Christ can heal all wounds," she said. "Let God take this burden from you now. I'm here for you. You don't have to carry this alone anymore. Neither of us will ever get over losing Zach, but I'd like to let the Atonement heal us now. We get to remember those people we've loved and lost, but it doesn't have to be all bad. Let's focus on the good memories."

"I can't tell you how much I want to do that," he said.

"You can, sweetheart. Oh, you can."

He held her close, breathing her in.

"When I saw that wall of flame close off my sight to you, I felt something horrible inside."

"And what was that?" she asked.

"I thought I'd never see you again. That I'd lose you, just like I lost Zach. And I didn't want to die without telling you that I loved you."

She made a small sound, like a tearful laugh of joy. "Oh, Sean! Do you know how long I've waited to hear you say that? Do you really mean it?"

"I do, sweetheart. I've realized that we're better off being together than being lonely apart. We have to live for each other. We have to trust each other."

"Yes, Sean. It's about time you realized that. And it's time I realized it, too." She whispered the words against his ear, snuggling closer to his warmth.

"I almost can't believe this is really happening."

"Well, it is," she said. "You asked me to trust you. And now I'm asking you to trust me. Can you do that, darling?"

He went very still. "Yes, Tess. I trust you, too."

She kissed his neck as though she never wanted to let go.

After a few moments he spoke softly. "Matt and I went to see Gavin last night."

She quirked her brows. "You did?"

"Yeah, he's back at home with his grandpa. He's still carrying a chip on his shoulder as big as Texas, but we told him we wouldn't give up on him. We invited him back to our Scout meetings. We made sure he knew he still has friends who care about him. And that's when I realized something else."

"What's that?" Her eyes softened as she listened intently.

"I realized that I was willing to fight for that lost boy, but I'd given up on myself. And I knew I couldn't do that. God wouldn't want that. If I wanted to teach Gavin and Matt about repentance and forgiveness, then I had to set an example for them. I had to forgive myself for what happened to Zach."

"Yes. Oh, yes," she said.

"I've decided to leave the hotshot crew," he said. "I've asked Jared Marshall if he can give me a desk job somewhere. Apparently Tim Wixler is retiring at the end of December. Jared said I could have his job if I want it. He'll make me his assistant fire management officer anytime I want the job."

She drew back and met his eyes. "Would a desk job make you happier?"

He tightened his hold around her. "I thought I should leave the crew so that I never caused anyone's death again. I promised myself that I'd leave just as soon as I fulfilled my promise to Zach."

"And what promise is that?" she asked.

"When you first joined the hotshot crew, I gave Zach my vow that I'd do everything in my power to keep you safe on the fireline. That I wouldn't let anything bad happen to you ever."

"Well, you've certainly kept your word," she said. "But you didn't cause anyone's death. And I don't care where you work, as long as you're happy and we're together. I know you're good at your job. There's none better. And the hotshot crew benefits from your leadership. You've done a great job keeping them safe. They rely on you, Sean."

He arched one brow. "Do you really mean that?"

She gave one decisive nod. "I do."

He released a cleansing sigh. "Then I guess it doesn't matter if I stay or go."

"That's right. You should do what makes you the happiest."

"All right, then I'll tell Jared that I want to stay right here with the Minoa Hotshots. And if he's smart, he'll hold Tim Wixler's job open until you graduate with your master's degree in the spring and then hire you as his assistant FMO."

She looked up at him, her eyelashes spiked by tears. "Do you think he would do that?"

"I do. It's certainly worth asking him."

"That job would make me your boss," she teased.

He flashed a wide smile. "I don't mind."

"It would also mean that we could stay right here in Minoa," she said. "But no matter where we might go, I'll always follow you. No jobs are worth more than what we share together. I love you, Sean. You're not pushing me away anymore. You can be as mean and nasty as you want, but I'm not leaving. You're stuck with me. For good this time. Got it?"

He gave a shuddering laugh. "I've got it, Tessie. I'm so sorry for ever breaking up with you."

"Then why did you?" she asked.

"Because I felt responsible for Zach's death and I thought you deserved better than to be married to the man who got your brother killed. I feared that one day you would blow up and leave me. I feared you would come to despise me. And I didn't want a divorce for us."

"You didn't get Zach killed. He was just a firefighter who lost his life in the line of duty. It happened. In my heart, you're both heroes, because you put your lives on the line to save others." Her voice was filled with compassion.

He contemplated her words for several moments. How he wanted to believe her. "I think I'll always feel responsible somehow. But when I was trying to save Dwight Connor's life during that fire a few days ago, I realized I wasn't in control of anything. God was. Only He could save us. And so I prayed. And I felt absolute peace wash over me. It was amazing, but I know God was there, directing me in what I should do. He kept us all safe."

She gave a hoarse laugh. "Oh, Sean. I don't doubt it at all."

"I also want you to know that I visited with my doctor yesterday," he said.

"Well, of course you did. You just got out of the hospital."

"No, I mean my psychiatrist. He's helping me work through my PTSD and survivor's guilt. It won't happen overnight, but I'm committed to getting better."

She released a slow breath and nodded, her expression soft and accepting. "I'm so glad. I've been very worried about you."

He lifted a hand and rested it on the counter to steady himself. "I was in denial for a long time. I didn't want to accept that I had a problem, that I had PTSD and couldn't fix it on my own. But you helped me realize that I needed outside help. I know it sounds odd, but I feel better now than I have in a year, and it's all because of you."

She shook her head. "No, Sean. I should have been more supportive from the start. I should have realized you pushed me away not because of anything you had done, but simply because you couldn't accept that you couldn't save Zach. So you blamed yourself."

"There wasn't anything you could have done," he said. "I had to figure it out by myself. I had to seek help on my own. And I've finally done that. But I almost lost you in the process."

"No, I'm still here."

"I hope so," he said. "I don't want to lose you, Tessa.

I love you and want you in my life. Nothing's more important to me than being with you."

Her eyes shimmered with happiness. "I've waited a long, lonely time to hear you say that."

"I'm just sorry it took me so long." A sudden lightness filled his heart. As though Zach was telling him to finally lay this burden down and live again. That he could finally be happy.

With Tessa.

She kissed him deeply, holding nothing back. And when they finally drew in a breath, he looked into her eyes and felt deep, abiding joy. They'd gone through a tremendous trial, but God had brought them through. The exhilaration and peace he felt was exquisite and complete.

"I suppose you'll want me to marry you now," he teased her, hoping she said yes.

She laughed, the sound high and sweet. "Of course I do. It's about time. The sooner, the better. We should have already gotten married last winter, so we've got to make up for lost time."

He pulled her close, welcoming her softness. Leaning his head down, he brushed the tip of his nose against hers. "Yes, it's time. You're right, of course."

"I usually am," she quipped.

He smiled, his heart overflowing with contentment. "Just name the date and I'll be there."

Her eyes locked with his as though she could see deep into his heart. Her gaze was filled with the tenderness and love he craved more than the air he breathed.

"I'll call Mom and we'll start making plans. She'll be thrilled. I love you, Sean."

"That's all I wanted to hear," he said.

He kissed her again, and no more words were needed. Not now. Not when they'd found their joy. Their happiness. Their love. It was here, in each other's arms. Together. Forever.

* * * * *

If you enjoyed this book, pick up the first
MEN OF WILDFIRE *story from Leigh Bale!*

HER FIREFIGHTER HERO

And don't miss these other books by Leigh Bale:

FALLING FOR THE FOREST RANGER
HEALING THE FOREST RANGER
THE FOREST RANGER'S RETURN
THE FOREST RANGER'S CHRISTMAS
THE FOREST RANGER'S RESCUE

Available now from Love Inspired!

Find more great reads at www.LoveInspired.com

Dear Reader,

In this story, Sean Nash has lost his best friend while fighting a wildfire. Even though it was no one's fault, Sean blames himself, suffering from post-traumatic stress disorder and survivor's guilt. In the process, he has pushed away Tessa, his fiancée, and refused to seek help for his sickness. It takes a lot of faith and patience for Sean to finally hand his burdens over to the Lord and let go of his pain.

When we face difficulties in our lives, it's so easy to blame others. It's easy to blame ourselves. Sometimes this is justified and sometimes it's not. But hating ourselves or others and holding a grudge never helps the situation. It does nothing more than canker our hearts and spirits. And that's not what our Heavenly Father wants for us. Through the Atonement, we have the healing power of repentance and can be forgiven of our sins. Through the power of faith, we can receive the strength we need to move forward with happy, productive lives. We need to trust that God is the great equalizer and will make everything right for us. His judgments are pure and will bring justice to every wrong.

I hope you enjoy reading this story and I invite you to visit my website at *www.LeighBale.com* to learn more about my books.

May you find peace in the Lord's words!
Leigh Bale

COMING NEXT MONTH FROM
Love Inspired®

Available April 18, 2017

A READY-MADE AMISH FAMILY
Amish Hearts • by Jo Ann Brown

As a minister, blacksmith and guardian to two sets of twins, widower Isaiah Stoltzfus needs help! Hiring Clara Ebersol as a nanny is his answer—and the matchmakers' solution to his single-dad life. It'll take four adorable children to show them that together they'd make the perfect family.

THE BULL RIDER'S HOMECOMING
Blue Thorn Ranch • by Allie Pleiter

Luke Buckton left Blue Thorn Ranch determined to become Texas's next rodeo star—leaving high school love Ruby Sheldon behind. When an injury sidelines him and she becomes his physical therapist, Ruby will help the reckless cowboy back into the saddle—but can she let him back into her heart?

THE BACHELOR'S TWINS
Castle Falls • by Kathryn Springer

Bachelor Liam Kane is content with his life—until Anna Leighton's precocious twin daughters turn it upside down. Suddenly he's playing dad...and falling for their mom. Can Liam convince her to let go of the secrets from her past so they can have a future together?

THEIR SURPRISE DADDY
Grace Haven • by Ruth Logan Herne

Big-city businessman Cruz Maldonado returns home to look after his late cousin's two children, never expecting he'd have to share guardianship with beautiful schoolteacher Rory Gallagher—or that their partnership would turn into love.

THE NANNY BARGAIN
Hearts of Hunter Ridge • by Glynna Kaye

Concerned for his orphaned twin half brothers who reside with their grandparents, Sawyer Banks recruits Tori Janner as their nanny—and to provide intel. Tori wants no part in spying, yet after spending time with the boys and their brother, she starts to long for something else—to become a mother and wife.

THE DAD NEXT DOOR
by Kat Brookes

After inheriting a house from her father, Claire Conley makes plans to turn it into a foster home. She doesn't have time for the single dad next door. But she can't turn away from Joe Sheehan's plea for help with his daughter—or the unexpected feelings he causes in her heart.

LOOK FOR THESE AND OTHER LOVE INSPIRED BOOKS WHEREVER BOOKS ARE SOLD, INCLUDING MOST BOOKSTORES, SUPERMARKETS, DISCOUNT STORES AND DRUGSTORES. LICNM0417

Get 2 Free Books,
Plus 2 Free Gifts—
just for trying the Reader Service!

YES! Please send me 2 FREE Love Inspired® Romance novels and my 2 FREE mystery gifts (gifts are worth about $10 retail). After receiving them, if I don't wish to receive any more books, I can return the shipping statement marked "cancel." If I don't cancel, I will receive 6 brand-new novels every month and be billed just $5.24 for the regular-print edition or $5.74 each for the larger-print edition in the U.S., or $5.74 each for the regular-print edition or $6.24 each for the larger-print edition in Canada. That's a saving of at least 13% off the cover price. It's quite a bargain! Shipping and handling is just 50¢ per book in the U.S. and 75¢ per book in Canada.* I understand that accepting the 2 free books and gifts places me under no obligation to buy anything. I can always return a shipment and cancel at any time. Even if I never buy another book, the 2 free books and gifts are mine to keep forever.

Please check one:
- ☐ Love Inspired Romance Regular-Print (105/305 IDN GLQC)
- ☐ Love Inspired Romance Larger-Print (122/322 IDN GLQD)

Name _____ (PLEASE PRINT)

Address _____ Apt. #

City _____ State/Province _____ Zip/Postal Code

Signature (if under 18, a parent or guardian must sign)

Mail to the **Reader Service**:
IN U.S.A.: P.O. Box 1867, Buffalo, NY 14240-1867
IN CANADA: P.O. Box 611, Fort Erie, Ontario L2A 9Z9

Want to try two free books from another line?
Call 1-800-873-8635 today or visit www.ReaderService.com.

*Terms and prices subject to change without notice. Prices do not include applicable taxes. Sales tax applicable in N.Y. Canadian residents will be charged applicable taxes. Offer not valid in Quebec. This offer is limited to one order per household. Books received may not be as shown. Not valid for current subscribers to Love Inspired Romance books. All orders subject to credit approval. Credit or debit balances in a customer's account(s) may be offset by any other outstanding balance owed by or to the customer. Please allow 4 to 6 weeks for delivery. Offer available while quantities last.

Your Privacy—The Reader Service is committed to protecting your privacy. Our Privacy Policy is available online at www.ReaderService.com or upon request from the Reader Service.

We make a portion of our mailing list available to reputable third parties that offer products we believe may interest you. If you prefer that we not exchange your name with third parties, or if you wish to clarify or modify your communication preferences, please visit us at www.ReaderService.com/consumerchoice or write to us at Reader Service Preference Service, P.O. Box 9062, Buffalo, NY 14240-9062. Include your complete name and address.

LII7R

SPECIAL EXCERPT FROM

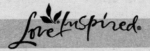

As a minister, blacksmith and guardian to two sets of twins, widower Isaiah Stoltzfus needs help! Hiring Clara Ebersol as a nanny is his answer—and the matchmakers' solution to his single-dad life. It'll take four adorable children to show them that together they'd make the perfect family.

Read on for a sneak preview of
A READY-MADE AMISH FAMILY
by *Jo Ann Brown,*
available May 2017 from Love Inspired!

"What's bothering you, Isaiah?" Clara asked when he remained silent.

"I assumed you'd talk to me before you made any decisions for the *kinder.*" As soon as the words left his lips, he realized how petty they sounded.

"I will, if that's what you want. But you hired me to take care of them. I can't do that if I have to wait to talk to you about everything."

He nodded. "I know. Forget I said that."

"We're trying to help the twins, and there are bound to be times when we rub each other the wrong way."

"I appreciate it." He did. She could have quit; then what would he have done? Finding someone else and disrupting the *kinder* who were already close to her would be difficult. "Why don't you tell me about these letters you and the twins were writing?"

"They are a sort of circle letter with their family. From what they told me earlier, they don't know any of them well, and I doubt their *aenti* and grandparents know much about

LIEXP0417

them. This way, they can get acquainted, so when the *kinder* go to live with whomever will be taking them, they won't feel as if they're living with strangers."

He was astonished at her foresight. He'd been busy trying to get through each day, dealing with his sorrow and trying not to upset the grieving *kinder*. He hadn't given the future much thought. Or maybe he didn't want to admit that one day soon the youngsters would leave Paradise Springs. His last connection to his best friend would be severed. The thought pierced his heart.

Clara said, "If you'd rather I didn't send out the letters—"

"Send them," he interrupted and saw shock widening her eyes. "I'm sorry. I didn't mean to sound upset."

"But you are."

He nodded. "Upset and guilty. I can't help believing that I'm shunting my responsibilities off on someone else. I want to make sure Melvin's faith in me as a substitute *daed* wasn't misplaced. The twins deserve a *gut daed*, but all they have is me."

"You're doing fine under the circumstances."

"You mean when the funeral was such a short time ago?"

"No, I mean when every single woman in the district is determined to be your next wife, and your deacon is egging them on."

In spite of himself, Isaiah chuckled quietly. Clara's teasing was exactly what he needed. Her comments put the silliness into perspective. If he could remember that the next time Marlin or someone else brought up the topic of him marrying, maybe he could stop making a mess of everything. He hoped so.

Don't miss
A READY-MADE FAMILY by Jo Ann Brown,
available May 2017 wherever
Love Inspired® books and ebooks are sold.

www.LoveInspired.com

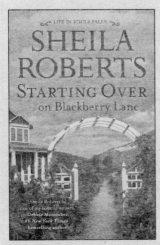